In Search of the Black Rose

Carolyn Keene
AR B.L.: 4.7
Points: 5.0   MG

Nancy Drew
Mystery Stories

Available from Simon & Schuster

In Search of the Black Rose

As Nancy and Bess passed the pub, Nancy spotted a shadow darting down another street. She shifted into high gear, plunging into the twisted back alley.

Nancy lurched around a turn and halted. A small wooden door was set in the wall. She hadn't noticed it before. Could their pursuer have gone in there?

As she hesitated, she heard a scraping sound above her head. She looked upward, just as Bess reeled around the corner.

Bess let out a scream. "Nancy—look out!"

A chunk of stone toppled off the wall—right toward Nancy.

NANCY DREW® 137

IN SEARCH OF THE BLACK ROSE

CAROLYN KEENE

Aladdin Paperbacks
New York   London   Toronto   Sydney   Singapore

This book is a work of fiction. Any references to historical events, real people, or real locales are used fictitiously. Other names, characters, places, and incidents are the product of the author's imagination, and any resemblance to actual events or locales or persons, living or dead, is entirely coincidental.

First Aladdin Paperbacks edition August 2002
First Minstrel edition June 1997

Copyright © 1997 by Simon & Schuster, Inc.

ALADDIN PAPERBACKS
An imprint of Simon & Schuster
Children's Publishing Division
1230 Avenue of the Americas
New York, NY 10020

Printed in the United States of America

10 9 8 7

NANCY DREW and NANCY DREW MYSTERY STORIES are registered trademarks of Simon & Schuster, Inc.

ISBN 0-671-00051-9

Contents

1

Trouble at High Table

"Wow—get a look at that rude gargoyle!" George Fayne exclaimed. Craning her neck, she peered at a carved face leering down from a nearby stone wall.

Nancy Drew chuckled. "George," she said, "you're so busy staring up at these old buildings, I'm afraid you're going to trip."

"Besides, you're definitely missing the main sights of Oxford University," added George's cousin, Bess Marvin. She nodded toward a pair of young men in jeans, strolling across the stone-paved courtyard in the direction of the three friends. Bess fluffed her long blond hair and threw them a winning smile. "English guys are definitely the cutest in the world."

Nancy gave Bess a swift nudge in the ribs. "We're not here to flirt, either," she said. "Dad said to

1

meet him at the Senior Common Room. Can either of you see a sign saying where that is?"

The three eighteen-year-old Americans stood, puzzled, in the main courtyard of Oxford's Boniface College. Dark-haired, athletic George grabbed a stone pillar, part of a cloistered walkway, and swung around it idly. Exasperated, Nancy ran her fingers through her shoulder-length red-blond hair.

"Are you girls lost?" a voice with an English accent boomed from behind them. They turned to see a stout middle-aged man with a bushy gray mustache and wire-rimmed glasses. Over his gray tweed jacket he wore a loose robe of flimsy black cotton.

"We're looking for the Senior Common Room," Nancy explained. "I'm supposed to meet my dad there—Carson Drew. We're guests of Derek Shaw, a law professor here. This is Boniface College, isn't it?"

"Indeed it is," the man answered heartily. "And I'm looking forward to meeting your father, the noted American lawyer. I'm Edgar Cole."

Wondering who Edgar Cole could be, Nancy shook his hand. "I'm Nancy Drew, and this is Bess Marvin and George Fayne. They've come over to England with my father and me for a vacation."

Mr. Cole shook their hands briskly. "So nice to meet you," he said. "Well. This way, then. . . ." He darted through an archway into a narrow, unlit corridor. Nancy and her friends followed.

2

After bustling up a short flight of stairs and down another hall, Mr. Cole stopped at a massive oak door with iron bolts and hinges. He thrust open the heavy door. "After you, my dears," he said.

Nancy, Bess, and George walked into a roomy, wood-paneled parlor, with thick carpeting and brocade armchairs. After the dark corridor and stairway, Nancy was surprised at how bright and elegant the room was. At the far end, a large bay window overlooked a lush garden. Beyond was a grand view of the town of Oxford, full of picturesque stone spires and gables and towers.

Around a side table, where cool drinks and predinner snacks were set out, a dozen men and women were gathered. All of them wore the same loose black robes as Mr. Cole. "What is this, some kind of cult?" Bess murmured nervously to Nancy.

"I think you'll find this is the Senior Common Room," Mr. Cole said. "Derek, I found these guests of yours wandering about."

One of the black-robed men turned around. Relieved, Nancy recognized her father's friend, Derek Shaw, a tall, thin man with unruly black hair.

"Hi, Mr. Shaw," Nancy said brightly.

Mr. Shaw gave a little wave. "Hello, Nancy," he replied. "And these two must be the famous George and Bess."

"Glad to see you're not impostors," Mr. Cole said to the girls. "I'll leave them to you, shall I, Derek?" Then he bustled over to another group of people.

"I see you've met the master of Boniface," Mr. Shaw said with a wry grin.

"Have we?" Bess asked, confused.

"So that's who Edgar Cole is," Nancy said. "I should have known. That's why he acts like he owns the place."

"He owns Boniface College?" George asked.

"Not really," Mr. Shaw said. "The master of a college is like the principal."

"Is that why he wears that black coat?" George asked, glancing over at Mr. Cole.

Mr. Shaw chuckled, raising his arms to show off his own robe. "No. Every member of the college—both the faculty and the students—must wear these academic gowns to college functions. Students don't have to wear them to dinner anymore, but we dons do."

"Dons?" Nancy asked.

"That's the Oxford term for 'professor,'" Mr. Shaw explained.

"Mr. Shaw, maybe you can tell me," Bess said. "I thought we were at Oxford University, but now everyone's calling this Boniface College."

"Boniface College is part of the university," Mr. Shaw explained. "Oxford's a collection of separate colleges, each with its own teachers, students, and walled campus. It's been so ever since Oxford was founded, back in the Middle Ages. Of course, Boniface is one of the newer colleges—it wasn't founded until 1674."

"That's old enough," George declared.

"I hope we haven't missed Dad," Nancy said. "He stayed at our hotel to phone his office while we took a walk around. He said he'd meet us here."

"Oh, I saw Carson downstairs," Mr. Shaw said. "I took him for a stroll in the Fellows' Garden—a special privilege, since only we dons have keys. But then a young lady joined us and stole him away from me." He led them to the window, where they could look down into the beautiful walled garden.

Nancy peered out, searching for her father amid the blooming roses and hollyhocks. Her eyes lit up as she spotted him beside a dark-haired teenage girl. "It's Pippa!" she exclaimed, waving through the window. Pippa and Mr. Drew looked up, waved back, and headed for the garden gate.

Nancy turned to George and Bess with an excited smile. "You remember I told you about Pippa Shaw, when the Shaws visited us in River Heights last summer? I hoped I'd see her on this trip."

"Ordinarily Pippa's away at boarding school, but she asked to make a special trip home this week," Mr. Shaw said, eyes twinkling. "Was it you she wanted to see so badly, Nancy? I thought she was just eager to hear your father's lecture to the Common Law Society on Friday evening."

"Sure," Nancy said, joking along with Mr. Shaw. "I'll bet she's fascinated by the topic of American inheritance laws."

The door to the Senior Common Room swung

open, and Pippa Shaw came in, Mr. Drew close behind. "Hi, Nan," Carson Drew said, leaning over to give his daughter a fond kiss. "Remember Pippa?"

"Do I ever!" Nancy replied, giving her English friend a quick hug.

While Mr. Shaw introduced Carson Drew around to the other dons, Nancy introduced Pippa to her two River Heights friends. The four of them chatted while they sipped sodas and nibbled on cheese crackers.

"Father says you'll be in Oxford for five days," Pippa said. "Do you have any special plans?"

"I want to do some cross-country hiking," George said. "I read that the Cotswold Hills are the place to go for that."

"Oh, yes, there are some super walking trails there," Pippa said. "A bit hilly, but brilliant views."

"While you're out working up a sweat, I think I'll just hang around Oxford trying to meet some students," Bess said. "You're so lucky to live here, Pippa. These guys are real hunks!"

Pippa grinned. "There are some smashing guys in college right now. When we go into the dining hall, you can look them over. Too bad we have to sit up at the high table, with the boring old dons. But at least it gives us a front-row seat."

"Speaking of front-row seats," Nancy said, "I hope we can go to London for some theater. There's

6

a new play I've heard about—*The Monkey Puzzle*, by Dame Gwyneth Davies. She's my all-time favorite mystery writer. Or maybe I should say she *was* my favorite. She died a couple of months ago, you know."

"She died?" Bess looked dismayed.

"Well, she was seventy-five years old," Pippa said. "She died of natural causes in her sleep. But the news hit the papers the day before the play opened, and there was ever so much publicity. Oddly enough, that made the play a hit."

"It would have been a hit anyway," a crisp British voice broke in beside Pippa's elbow. Startled, the girls turned to see a gray-haired woman in a wheelchair. Her piercing dark eyes flashed as she wheeled forward.

"Oh, Miss Innes," Pippa said. "I didn't know you were—"

"Gwyneth Davies wasn't just a good mystery writer, she was a great writer, period," Miss Innes said, briskly smoothing down her black gown. "And a brilliant philosophy don, even if she did teach at St. Cyril's College and not Boniface."

"Miss Innes, these are my friends from America—Nancy Drew, Bess Marvin, and George Fayne," Pippa said. "Miss Innes teaches history here. She was Dame Gwyneth's closest friend, weren't you?"

"For years," Miss Innes said, "ever since the days of the Puzzlers. We were the only women in the

7

club—all the others were men. Philosophers, mathematicians, even a scientist or two . . . now, *there* was a group of people who knew how to use their minds. We'd sit up till all hours, making up complex riddles and logic problems to confound one another."

"And scavenger hunts, too," Nancy added eagerly. "I remember reading about them in Dame Gwyneth's second book, *Murder by the Fireside.*"

Miss Innes stared at Nancy with shrewd approval. "Very good. You're a fan, I see."

"I've read every one of her books," Nancy said.

"Nancy's a detective herself," Pippa added. "Back home in America, she's solved all sorts of cases that have even stumped the police."

Miss Innes drew herself up stiffly. In a choked voice, she said, "A *detective?*"

Nancy blushed. She never liked to draw attention to her success as an amateur detective. "Yes, ma'am," she answered. "A few times I've stumbled onto a case I was able to figure out." She kicked Pippa's shoe to keep her friend quiet.

"Not a very ladylike occupation, I'd say," Miss Innes muttered. Then she spun her wheelchair around and left.

"What's with her?" George asked.

Pippa sighed and shrugged. "I don't know," she replied. "She's always been a bit eccentric. Father says she took Dame Gwyneth's death very hard. Still, why should she care if Nancy solves crimes?"

A deep-toned bell began to ring from some nearby tower. As if on cue, all the dons set down their drinks and started moving toward a small door in a side wall. "On to the hall for dinner," Pippa said. "Now you can get a look at those students, Bess."

After passing through the door, Nancy and her friends entered a long, magnificent room paneled in dark wood. The arched ceiling had grand carved rafters, and stained-glass windows were set into one side wall. Three banquet tables stretched the length of the hall, and a couple of hundred students stood by them, waiting to sit. The dons and their guests took seats at a fourth table on a low platform built across the top of the hall. At the far end, an elaborately carved balcony overhung the entrance.

Nancy had hoped that she and her friends could sit together at dinner, but the master, Mr. Cole, had other plans. Nancy found herself seated next to a tall thirtyish man with glasses, Mark Sunderwirth, who told her he taught French. Down the table, she spotted her father seated next to the master. George sat on the other side of the master's wife, a robust blond woman. Bess was seated at the far end of the table beside Mr. Shaw.

White-coated waiters flocked in, bearing steaming platters of roast beef and Yorkshire pudding. Nancy tasted hers. "Umm—better than most college food," she remarked to Mr. Sunderwirth.

"Oh, yes," he said pleasantly. "A Boniface alum

9

owns England's largest chain of grocery stores, and he donates all our food. We're known to serve the best meals in the university. No one ever passes up an invitation to dine at Boniface."

"Well, someone's missing a Boniface dinner," Nancy said, nodding to the empty chair on the other side of her.

Mr. Sunderwirth frowned. "That should be Dorothy Innes's place," he said. "She's our medieval history fellow. But I thought I saw her in the Common Room earlier."

"She was there, all right," Nancy said. "I chatted with her, but I didn't see her leave the room."

"She's a funny old bird," Mr. Sunderwirth said. Now he sounded unconcerned. "Perhaps she simply didn't feel up to dinner. Her health hasn't been all that good lately."

"Is that why she's in a wheelchair?" Nancy asked.

"She's been in a chair ever since I was a student here at Boniface," he said, spearing a chunk of rare roast beef on his fork. "The word is that she had a riding accident when she was young."

"She was very good friends with Dame Gwyneth Davies, wasn't she?" Nancy said.

"The late Dame Gwyneth," Mr. Sunderwirth said. "I've never read any of her books, I must confess. I'm not a mystery fan. But I did see *The Monkey Puzzle* last week—a super play. Have you seen it?"

"No, but I'd like to," Nancy said.

"They were both members of the famous Puzzlers," Mr. Sunderwirth said. He gave her a sly sideways glance. "Do you know about the club?"

"Yes, I do," Nancy said. "They used to have big banquets, where they would ask each other complicated riddles and logic problems and—"

"Yes, and they were mad about practical jokes, too," Mr. Sunderwirth interrupted, sitting up eagerly. "Once they invented a fictional professor to apply for a post at St. Cyril's. They wrote fake references for him, even hired an actor to show up for his job interview. They did such a good job that the bloke was actually hired. Quite an embarrassment for St. Cyril's when the truth came out. Then there was the time they . . ."

Mr. Sunderwirth went on at length, relating tales of the Puzzlers' antics. From the gleam in his eyes, Nancy could tell he was a bit fanatical on the subject. She was interested at first, but soon her attention wandered. *I must be tired from our long trip,* she told herself, stifling a yawn.

"Oh, look—gooseberry tart for dessert!" Mr. Sunderwirth announced suddenly.

"Gooseberry?" Nancy asked, rousing herself.

"One of my favorites," he replied. A waiter cleared their dinner plates and set down a pie filled with what looked like overgrown green grapes.

"I've never eaten gooseberries—" Nancy began.

She halted in midsentence as a blur of motion in

11

the balcony over the entrance caught her eye. She heard a faint twang and saw a billow of black cloth behind the railing.

An arrow came whistling down the length of the huge dining hall. *Zing!* The shaft quivered as the sharp arrowhead struck and pierced the ancient oak table—right in front of Nancy's plate.

2

A Mysterious Message

A stunned hush fell over the dining hall. Nancy leaped to her feet. The arrowhead must be very sharp to pierce the thick table, she thought. If the mysterious archer had aimed a fraction of an inch higher, she could have been badly wounded—or worse.

Had the arrow hit its mark? Or had it missed the intended target?

She looked up at the balcony again, but she couldn't see anyone. "Quick, how do you get up to that balcony?" she asked Mr. Sunderwirth in a low, urgent voice.

"It's called a minstrel's gallery," he said. "In the Middle Ages, singers entertaining a lord's banquet would sit there. Of course, Boniface has never had actual minstrels singing—it's only an architectural detail—"

13

"Whatever it's called, how do you get there?" Nancy asked. "I have to find out who shot that arrow."

"Will everyone please be seated?" Mr. Cole called out from the center of the high table. "Luckily no one has been hurt by this mystery missile. Go back to your gooseberry tart, please." He shot a commanding glance at Nancy.

Reluctantly, she sank back into her chair. "Someone could have been hurt," she said as a murmur of conversation swelled again through the dining hall. "I'm surprised nobody's concerned."

Against the master's orders, Carson Drew left his seat and came to crouch beside Nancy's chair. "Are you all right?" he asked anxiously.

"I'm fine, Dad—just a little shaken," Nancy said. "And baffled, too, I have to admit."

"Oh, it's probably just another prank," Mr. Sunderwirth said, digging into his pie.

"Another prank?" Nancy asked. "Does this sort of thing happen a lot?"

"Oxford is full of clever young people who enjoy a bit of mischief now and then," he answered with a shrug. "There are always pranks. The trouble is, they're never clever pranks. Not like in the days of the Puzzlers."

Nancy turned away before Mr. Sunderwirth could launch into his favorite topic again. "Is that a message?" her father asked, pointing to the arrow.

Nancy looked back in surprise. She hadn't even noticed the paper wrapped tightly around the

14

arrow's shaft. Reaching out, she grasped the shaft and pulled it out of the oak table. As the arrowhead came free, it made a resounding *poing.*

Nancy unrolled a sheet of ivory-colored paper. Spreading it out on the table, she saw what looked like an advertising flyer:

The Boniface Players
present
Tragedie of the Black Knight
a 17th-century melodrama
starring Simon Coningsby as the Knight
7 P.M., Thursday through Sunday
Boniface Garden

Nancy became aware that Mr. Sunderwirth was leaning over her shoulder, reading. When he saw her look at him, he sat back quickly. "Those posters are plastered all over town," he said, waving his hand. "It's the college's summer play, opening this week. Simon Coningsby is Boniface's budding star. He's quite talented, actually—but not as talented as he thinks he is. He's better suited to romantic comedy than heavy drama like *Tragedie of the Black Knight.*"

"Is he here tonight?" Nancy asked.

"Over there." He pointed out a young man at one of the long student tables nearby. Slim and pale, with light brown hair, he was very good-looking, Nancy had to admit.

"This was probably just a publicity stunt advertising Coningsby's new star turn," Mr. Sunderwirth said. "Typical. The lad does have a flair for the dramatic."

"He couldn't have shot that arrow," Nancy said. "If he had, he wouldn't be back in his seat already."

Carson Drew patted Nancy's arm and rose to his feet. "I'd better go back and sit down before the master gets annoyed."

"But, Dad, I still think I should go check out that minstrel's gallery," Nancy said.

"Whoever shot the arrow is long gone by now," Mr. Sunderwirth remarked.

"I'll go up with you after dinner if you want to investigate," Carson Drew said. "Derek Shaw or Pippa can show us the way." He squeezed her shoulder, then walked back to his seat.

Nancy toyed with her dessert spoon. She sampled the pie, but after her recent close call, the sour taste of the gooseberries didn't sit well. Laying down her spoon, she turned her attention to Simon Coningsby. He sat leaning lazily over the table, his cheek on one hand. His glossy hair flopped down over his alert gray eyes.

Nancy wondered why Mr. Sunderwirth had been so quick to blame Simon Coningsby for shooting the arrow. It was true, though, that the young actor did seem totally unfazed by the incident. Was that because he'd known about it ahead of time? she wondered. Or was he simply unconcerned, like everybody else in the hall? It was hard to tell, she reasoned. If he was such a good actor, he could easily cover up his feelings.

Idly, Nancy held up the flyer that had been wrapped around the arrow to study it more closely. But as the light fell on the flyer from both sides, she noticed something new. There was writing on the other side, too.

Nancy flipped over the paper quickly. A note was scrawled there in red ink, in tiny, precise handwriting:

> *Look behind the black rose, in due time,*
> *And you'll avert a grievous crime.*

Nancy felt her heart leap. Was this message meant for her? If not, for whom? Mr. Sunderwirth certainly had been interested. Or could it have been meant for the missing Miss Innes?

She longed to share the note with someone—but only someone who would take it seriously. She leaned forward and craned her neck to catch Bess's attention, but Bess was deep in conversation with Mr. Shaw. She managed to catch George's eye, however, and signaled to her to meet right after dinner. With George sitting so close to the master, Nancy didn't want to reveal any more.

After carefully folding the note, Nancy slipped it into her lap. The summery pale blue skirt she was wearing didn't have pockets, so she tucked the paper into her waistband. Then she checked her watch impatiently. They'd sat down at seven P.M. It

17

was almost eight now. When would this dinner be over? Glancing at the students, she could tell they were eager to go, too, but apparently no one was supposed to get up until the master did.

Nancy let her eyes rove over the hall. The summer evening's late daylight fell through the diamond-patterned stained glass, casting wedges of pale color on the stone floor. A few portraits hung on the dark-paneled walls—either famous alumni or former masters, Nancy guessed. After glancing over the portraits, Nancy studied the intricate wood carving set at intervals along the walls.

She sat up straight and narrowed her eyes. A carved coat of arms was mounted below the fifth window on the left-hand wall. In the center of the crest was a rose, carved in black wood.

Was this the black rose that the mysterious rhyme referred to?

As Nancy began to feel for the note in her waistband, a stir rippled through the room. Looking down the table, she saw that the master had risen to his feet. With a swirl of his black gown, he strode down the platform, heading back to the Senior Common Room.

The rafters echoed with the sound of chairs and benches scooting back from the tables. Students were leaping up and racing for the doors. After stealing one more glance at the minstrel's gallery— still apparently empty—Nancy jumped up, too.

Mr. Sunderwirth turned to her as the crowd

moved along the platform. "Going to the Common Room for coffee?"

"Uh, I'm not sure," Nancy said. "I'd better check with my friends. You go ahead." He gave her an uneasy, questioning look, then went on.

Nancy found George waiting beside the door to the Common Room. "Bess and your dad are already in there," George explained. "I guess we're expected to stick around."

Nancy groaned. "No way—we've waited long enough," she said. "Maybe the master doesn't care if people go around shooting arrows at his guests, but I sure do!"

She pulled George aside and showed her the note that had been wrapped around the shaft. George's eyes opened wide. "'Look behind the black rose, in due time,/And you'll avert a grievous crime,'" she read aloud. "What crime do you think it's talking about, Nan?"

"No idea," Nancy said. "Maybe this is all a hoax. Still, it can't hurt to search that minstrel's gallery at some point. I know the mystery archer is gone by now, but we might find some clues."

"Which would help us figure out whether or not this is all a wild-goose chase," George said.

"I can't believe it is," Nancy said. "That arrow was carrying a specific message—either for me or for one of my dinner neighbors."

"But why all the mystery?" George asked.

"I don't know," Nancy said. "Maybe whoever

19

sent that note is being watched or is in some kind of trouble." She shrugged. "At any rate, I did see a black rose carved on the wall over there. We might as well take a closer look at it."

George and Nancy made their way across the dining hall, skirting the long tables. A crew of white-coated waiters, busy clearing the tables, eyed the girls suspiciously.

Standing below the wood carving, Nancy frowned. "It's higher up than I thought," she said. "We'll need a stepladder to reach it."

"Nan, I don't think these waiters want you snooping around," George said. "If you get a ladder and start prying at the woodwork—"

"Say, I was looking for you two," Pippa's voice broke in from behind them. "Admiring the carving? It's by Grinling Gibbons, a very famous woodcarver."

"Pippa—just the person I wanted," Nancy said. She told her about the note scrawled on the flyer.

Pippa frowned. "I don't think we should mess about with the woodwork—not without the master's permission," she said. "It's one of the college's most prized features."

Nancy sighed. "I'm sure he'll say the note was just a prank."

"You don't think he's covering up something, do you?" George asked.

"I doubt that," Pippa said. "But he certainly does like to put a smooth face on things. Public relations, and all that."

"All we have right now is a cryptic note from someone with a bizarre method of delivering messages," Nancy said. "But if we do find something, maybe the master will listen to us. I promise we won't hurt the wall in any way."

"Pippa, aren't you dying to find out what this riddle is all about?" George asked. "I know I am."

Pippa let out a sigh. "Of course I'm curious, too. Let me think. Mr. Austin, the college porter, might help us. He lives in the lodge by the college gate. He's a special chum of mine."

"Should we get Bess and your father?" George asked.

"Better not. I don't want the master to catch us and make us stay in the Common Room," Nancy said.

The three hurried to the gate lodge. Mr. Austin, a retired soldier with a hearty smile, found them a wooden stepladder, a small chisel, a hammer, and a flashlight, which he called a torch. Lugging the ladder, Nancy and her two friends stole quietly through the cloistered courtyard back to the hall.

The heavy oak doors were closed but not locked. Inside the hall, however, the lights had been turned off. "And here I am without my penlight," Nancy said. "Thank goodness Mr. Austin thought to give us this flashlight—I mean torch." Switching it on, she lit the way to the fifth window.

Pippa propped open the ladder. "Just tall enough," she said.

Nancy began to climb up. "Hurry, Nan," George

said, looking over her shoulder. "I hear the dons—they're still in the Common Room. We don't want them finding us here."

"I feel positively criminal." Pippa giggled.

From the top step, Nancy reached up to the carving. She took the chisel and edged it delicately around the rim of the crest. "It's a separate piece of wood, nailed on," she told the others.

"There could be a hiding place behind it," Pippa exclaimed. "Oh, I hope there is!"

Nancy held her breath and gently pried up the black rose crest.

3

The Search Heats Up

"Give me that flashlight, Pippa." Nancy reached down from the ladder.

Pippa handed it up. "Can you see anything under the crest?" she asked eagerly.

Nancy squinted as she trained the beam under the wood carving. "Not a thing," she said. "There's nothing here but smooth walnut planks." She pressed the crest back into place, feeling the nails ease back into the wood. "And it looks like they haven't been disturbed since the seventeenth century."

"Maybe what we're looking for was hidden in the seventeenth century," George said.

Nancy shook her head. "Then why would someone only be worried about it now? Besides, the note said we had to 'avert a grievous crime.' Whatever that crime is, if it started that long ago, how could we hope to prevent it now?"

"What if the secret is hidden behind the paneling itself?" George suggested.

Nancy began to tap the paneling. "There's no way the college would let us take apart the hall's paneling," Pippa said. "This room is a national historic landmark."

"There's no hollow space anyway," Nancy announced as she climbed down the stepladder. "Frankly, we don't even know if this is the black rose the riddle meant. We need stronger evidence. Maybe we'll find something in the minstrel's gallery that would prove—"

The door to the Senior Common Room popped open, letting a stream of light into the darkened hall. The three young women started in fear.

A figure loomed in the open doorway. "Ladies?" inquired the gruff voice of the master.

Nancy hastily shoved the stepladder into the shadows, out of sight. "Mr. Cole?" she replied. "We were just, uh, admiring the stained glass. It's so much easier to appreciate the colors when the lights aren't on."

"Yes, lovely indeed," the master said. "But the porter should be along to lock up any minute now. Why don't you join us in here?" He turned and went back into the Common Room.

"I'll see that Mr. Austin gets the ladder and tools back," Pippa whispered. "You go on in. No point in making the master suspicious."

"Thanks," Nancy whispered back. "Do you want to meet tomorrow morning? Ten o'clock, by the gate?"

"You bet," Pippa answered with an impish grin. "I've never helped solve a mystery before. Wild horses couldn't keep me away."

After making a token appearance in the Senior Common Room, Nancy signaled to her father that she was eager to go. Many of the dons were already leaving anyway. After saying good night to the master and to Mr. Shaw, the Drews, Bess, and George walked out through the college. It was a ten-minute stroll from there to their rambling hotel in north Oxford.

As they walked, Nancy, Bess, George, and Mr. Drew discussed the evening's intriguing events. "Too bad that wood carving didn't hold any answers," George said. "It seemed so logical. Why else would the archer send you the message right there in the dining hall?"

"We don't know for sure that the message was sent to me," Nancy said. "It could have been for Mr. Sunderwirth, maybe, or for Miss Innes—even though she wasn't there."

"But it urged you to look for something," Bess said. "You're a detective—neither of them is. You're the only one who really would look for the black rose. You said Mr. Sunderwirth didn't even take the incident seriously, and Miss Innes is in a wheelchair—she'd have a hard time prowling around."

"There's one way to find out what the message refers to," Carson Drew said. "Find the black rose. The rose is a common feature in medieval heraldry, as well as a frequent religious symbol. With all the ancient buildings and art objects in Oxford, there should be lots of roses around." He waved his hand at the old stone walls around them. "If anything, there may be too many. It might be like looking for a needle in a haystack."

"We need more information to go on," Nancy said. "But with Mr. Cole breathing down our necks, we couldn't search the minstrel's gallery tonight."

"Why are you scared of telling Edgar Cole what you're up to?" Mr. Drew said. "If you like, I'll speak to him tomorrow to get permission for you to search around the college. Let me show him the note—that should convince him."

"Thanks, Dad, that should help," Nancy said, handing over the note.

"Nancy, how is it that you turn up a mystery wherever you go?" Bess asked.

"This one practically flew into my lap," Nancy said wryly. "But I can't ignore the riddle. If there really is a 'grievous crime' we can prevent, we should do it—the sooner the better."

As Nancy, Bess, and George walked up Broad Street the next morning, they spotted Pippa waiting outside the Boniface College gates. From the way she was restlessly bouncing her foot against the great stone pillars, Nancy could tell she was eager to go searching for clues.

Pippa's face lit up when she saw them. "I thought you'd never get here," she called out.

"We walked my dad to the law library," Nancy said. "He still has research to do for his lecture Friday night. Then he's having lunch with some other law professors."

Pippa rolled her eyes. "And my father's tied up in classes all day," she added. "It's dreadfully frustrating. I wanted him to let us into the Fellows' Garden. Only the senior dons have keys."

"That's the garden you and Dad were walking in last night?" Nancy asked.

Pippa nodded. "Father unlocked the gate for us yesterday, but it's strictly off limits to everyone except college fellows—senior faculty members."

"It did look like a lovely garden," George said, "but I'm sure we can see it some other time."

"It's more urgent than that," Pippa said. "I had a bit of a brainstorm this morning, you see. The Fellows' Garden has ever so many rosebushes. What if our black rose is one of them?"

"Good idea," Nancy said. "We'll check it out as soon as your father can let us in. In the meantime, we have loads of other options to investigate. In fact, we'll need to split up if we want to cover everything."

"We've got a map of Oxford," George said to Pippa, pulling a large foldout map from the pocket of her denim jacket. "I didn't realize it, but there are more than thirty colleges here, not to mention university libraries and museums and parks. Is there somewhere we can sit to divide up the territory?"

"Let's go to the Junior Common Room," Pippa suggested, gesturing through the gates.

"The Common Room again?" Bess said, looking skeptical.

Pippa grinned. "The *Junior* Common Room this time—where the students hang out. I think you'll find it quite different from that stuffy old Senior Common Room."

Nancy and her friends followed Pippa through the gates, waving to Mr. Austin at the door of the lodge. "Normally, the college is only open to visitors between the hours of one and five P.M.," Pippa told Nancy and her friends. "And even then, unless you're a member of the university, you have to pay a small entrance fee of twenty-five pence. They always let me in, though, because they know me."

"So that's why we had to give our names to the guard in the lodge when we came in yesterday," Bess said. "I guess we were on his guest list."

"Yes," Pippa said. "There are so many tourists wandering around Oxford, it became quite a problem for the students and dons. So now most colleges limit access for the public."

Pippa swiftly led them across the main college quadrangle, through the cloistered courtyard, and around the corner of the dining hall. After passing through a small arched gateway, they came out onto a long stretch of smooth grass surrounded by a few flower beds and a wall of golden stone. At the far end of this yard, students were busy hammering together a structure of iron pipes.

"This is the college garden," Pippa said. "It's not as exclusive as the Fellows' Garden—anybody can walk here. They're building a stage for the summer play," she added, nodding toward the students.

"Tragedie of the Black Knight?" Nancy asked.

"Why, yes," Pippa said. "I gather you've seen the posters. They're all over town."

"The message on the arrow was written on one of those posters," Nancy reminded Pippa.

"So the archer probably just pulled a poster off the wall to write the message," Pippa said.

Halfway down the garden, Pippa took a quick turn through a small open doorway. It led into a narrow paved courtyard. On one side was the back of an old building, in the same golden stone as the rest of the college. On the other side was a modern building in gray concrete, jammed into a corner. "There isn't much room for the college to expand," Pippa said. "Nobody wants the historic old buildings torn down, and there are other colleges on both sides. The architect really had to work to fit this new dorm into that space, didn't he?"

She led them through the glass doors at the base

of the new building. Inside, another pair of glass doors stood open on their left. "Here's the Junior Common Room," Pippa announced.

Nancy and her friends stepped into the student lounge. With walls of painted concrete, it was as casual and modern as the Senior Common Room was formal and old-fashioned. The low-slung furniture was made of black leather and chrome. Two couches and several chairs were grouped around a TV set in one corner. A big bulletin board near the doors was plastered with flyers and notices. Magazines and newspapers lay scattered on a nearby table.

A pass-through opening in one wall led to a kitchenette next door. A college worker in a turquoise smock was serving coffee, tea, fruit, and cookies from the counter there. At Pippa's suggestion, each girl took a cup of tea.

"I'll fetch the biscuits," Pippa said.

"No biscuits for me, thanks," Bess said. "I'll just have a couple of cookies."

Pippa looked blank for a minute, then smiled. "Oh, I forgot—what we call biscuits are the same things you call cookies."

Bess rolled her eyes. "When am I ever going to get the hang of *English* English?"

Nancy, Bess, and George seated themselves at a nearby coffee table while Pippa went to the tea counter. Nancy noticed Bess staring across the room. "Wow, who's that?" Bess asked eagerly.

Nancy turned to look. "It's Simon Coningsby," she said. Hands in his pockets, the handsome young man was whistling and studying the bulletin board.

"Do you know him, Nan?" Bess asked.

"Not really," Nancy said. "Mr. Sunderwirth pointed him out to me last night. He's the star of the college play—I guess he plays the Black Knight."

"We should definitely get tickets to it, then," Bess said. "Like, tonight."

Almost as if he knew they had been talking about him, Simon Coningsby looked over. Tossing her blond hair, Bess flashed him a smile. He smiled back and began to cross the room toward them.

"Look, Nan, he's coming our way!" Bess whispered. "Can you introduce me to him?"

"I haven't been introduced to him myself," Nancy said. She traded amused glances with George.

"I say, have we met?" Simon Coningsby said as he reached their table. His rich voice and cultured accent made him sound already like a movie star, Nancy thought to herself.

Bess leaned back in her chair and gazed up at him. Her blue eyes sparkled. "No, but we could fix that," she said. "I'm Bess Marvin."

"Bess. I'm Simon," he said, shaking her hand. He held it for an extra moment as he stared intently down at her. "Charmed to meet you."

Bess seemed speechless for a minute, so George broke in. "I'm George Fayne, and this is Nancy

Drew," she said in a no-nonsense manner. "We're only visiting Oxford for a week. We're from America."

"I gathered as much when I heard you speak," Simon said. He finally dropped Bess's hand, but he continued to look only at her. "I noticed you all at high table last night. I asked about you. Three mystery women—nobody had a clue who you were, or what business brings you to Oxford."

Nancy decided this was a good opportunity to fish around for information. "Speaking of mysteries," she said to Simon, "what did you think of that arrow flying into the hall last night? Does that sort of thing happen often around here?"

"Arrow?" Simon tore his eyes from Bess and looked, confused, at Nancy.

"Tea time!" Pippa's voice broke in. She bustled up and plunked a tray full of teacups on the low table. "And guess what—I've met an old school chum. Nancy, Bess, George, this is Tony D'Souza. He graduated two years ago from my boarding school. We were on the gymnastics team together."

Nancy turned around to see a young man with straight black hair, dark eyes, and dusky skin, wearing jeans and a Boniface sweatshirt. He had been smiling pleasantly, but his expression froze when he saw Simon Coningsby standing there.

Out of the corner of her eye, Nancy noticed that Simon stiffened, too. His chin lifted sharply, and his shoulders hunched up.

"Hello, Simon," Tony said in a wary voice.

"Well, I see you don't need *me* to show you around Oxford, Bess," Simon said haughtily. "Perhaps we'll run into each other again sometime."

And without another word, Simon spun around and stalked off.

4

A Teacher in Trouble

"Well, what was all *that* about?" Pippa asked, dropping into a chair. "Why was he so rude, Tony?"

Tony clenched his jaw. "I've never been able to figure that bloke out," he muttered.

"Do you know Simon well?" Bess asked.

Tony squirmed slightly, looking uncomfortable. "I met him when I first came up to Oxford," he said. "He took me under his wing, introduced me around. He'd already been here a year, you see, and he knew absolutely everybody. He'd invite me to tea in his room, and we'd talk for hours. But then he dropped me—just like that." He snapped his fingers. "Now he'll pass me in the street and not even say hello."

"Maybe you got on his wrong side somehow," George said, lifting her teacup.

"I can't imagine how," Tony said with a sniff. "I truly liked him. He can be very charming company, you know."

"I can certainly see that," Bess said. She still looked dazzled from her encounter with Simon.

"Yes, but it's all put on," Tony said to her. "Don't get taken in by Simon Coningsby." His dark eyes narrowed.

Nancy observed Tony closely. Clearly, he and Simon had had a falling-out. But whose fault was it—Tony's or Simon's? And what had really been the cause of it?

"I was going to give my friends a tour of Oxford, Tony," Pippa said, changing the subject. "Would you like to join us?"

Tony ran a hand through his black hair. "Would I ever," he said. "Except that I haven't finished my paper for my session today with Miss Innes: Land reform in medieval France."

Nancy smiled. "Is that the same Miss Innes we met last night?" she asked. She bit into a cookie.

"The one and only," Pippa said. "She's Tony's tutor, his main teacher and adviser."

"She's brilliant," Tony said, "but she seems awfully distracted these days."

"I can see why, with her best friend dying and all," George said.

"Her best friend?" Tony raised an eyebrow.

"Oh, you know, Tony—Gwyneth Davies. The mystery writer," Pippa said. "She died a couple of months ago."

"Well, that's about when Miss Innes began acting so strangely," Tony said. "She seems quite on edge. Once while I was meeting with her in her rooms, the phone rang and she nearly jumped out of her skin. A couple of times, she's abruptly changed our meeting time at the last minute. And she'll stare out the window without listening while I'm reading my papers to her."

"Maybe that's because your papers are so boring," Pippa said. She reached over to swat Tony playfully.

Tony finally mustered a grin. "No doubt," he said. "In that case, I'd better get to work and make this next paper a little more interesting. It's lovely to meet you all. I'll ring you soon, Pippa." With a little wave, he headed for the door.

Nancy popped the rest of her cookie into her mouth and chewed thoughtfully. "I wonder what's up with Miss Innes," she said. "Tony says she hasn't been herself lately. And she sure did act weird yesterday evening when we met her. If the arrow in the hall was meant to carry a message to her—"

"But she wasn't even there," George said. "The archer must have been able to see that. I mean, you don't shoot a deadly weapon like an arrow without taking aim first."

"And that was no amateur shooting," Pippa said. "I've done some archery, and I know how difficult it would be to send an arrow that far and that straight."

Nancy drained her teacup. "We really should

check out that minstrel's gallery," she said. "Pippa, can you show us the way there?"

Pippa's face brightened. "I think so," she said. "I mean, even I can get confused in some back corners of the college—these buildings have been patched together so strangely over the years. But I'm sure we can find it."

The four of them went back out through the glass doors, across the cramped back courtyard, and into the college garden. Bess cast a wistful glance at the stage that was being built. The pipe skeleton had been finished, and now students were laying down thick boards on top. "I can't wait to see that play," she said.

"Just because Simon Coningsby's in it?" George teased her cousin.

Bess looked annoyed. "Well, he is handsome, and I'll bet he's great onstage. Is he, Pippa?"

"I've got no idea," Pippa said. "I've never seen him in anything. I'm not a student here, remember. I only know Tony because he went to my boarding school."

She turned through the garden gate and led them along the short, cobblestoned alley behind the dining hall. Soon they reached the arched doorway to the dining hall and stepped inside the cool, stone-paved vestibule.

"I hope the doors aren't locked," Bess said.

"They shouldn't be," Pippa said. "The students were here for breakfast, and lunch should be served

37

in another hour or so. But we don't want to go through the main doors, anyway."

Reaching the end of the vestibule, Pippa stopped in front of a small wooden door. She tried the doorknob. It wasn't locked. "Great," Pippa said, opening the door. "Here we go."

A narrow stone staircase led upward from the vestibule. Nancy went first. Reaching a tiny landing where the stairs turned sharply, Nancy looked above her. At the top of the stairs she could see the high, raftered ceiling of the dining hall.

They came out of the stairs into a narrow open space, about five feet wide and fifty feet long. The bare wooden floor matched the polished walls of the hall, and the wall on their left was covered with the same dark paneling. On their right, a waist-high wooden parapet divided the gallery from the main hall.

The dining hall lights were not turned on; the only light was a murky colored glow from the stained-glass windows. "Wish we had a torch," Pippa said.

"I've got my penlight," Nancy said, reaching into her purse. "But even in this light, I can tell there isn't much to see. Basically, this is a big wooden box hung halfway up the wall. A big *bare* wooden box."

George leaned over to inspect the elaborate carving on the outside of the parapet. "Do you think there are any black roses here?"

"Could be," Nancy said hopefully.

"Do you mean like that rose on the crest we saw last night?" Pippa asked. "I doubt it. Each of those crests on the dining hall's side walls is different. They represent coats of arms from the twelve noble families who helped found this college."

"I'll look anyway, while we're up here," George said. She threw one leg over the railing and braced herself to inspect the wood carving.

"Watch what you're doing, George," Bess said. Not nearly as athletic as her cousin, she had a healthy fear of heights.

"Where does that door go, Pippa?" Nancy asked, pointing to a small wooden door in the paneling on the gallery's back wall.

Pippa frowned. "I've got no idea."

Nancy strode to the door and grabbed the wooden doorknob. The door opened onto a carpeted second-floor corridor with doors on both sides.

Pippa peered over Nancy's shoulder. "Those look like dons' studies," she said. "Some dons live in apartments in college, and they meet with their students in their own sitting rooms. But dons who live out of college, like my father, are given studies in college where they can hold seminars."

Nancy walked a few steps down the corridor, inspecting the hand-lettered name cards mounted on each door. "Mr. A. Danchev, Mrs. M. Court, Mr. R. Bootle . . ." she read.

"I recognize those names," Pippa said. "These are definitely faculty studies."

"Anybody could have entered the minstrel's gallery from this wing, then," Nancy said. "Our archer could easily have slipped in and out with no one noticing."

The corridor ended at an ordinary stairway with worn carpeting. At the side of the landing, there was also a narrow elevator door. "It seems funny to have an elevator here," Nancy said. "The stairs don't go up any farther, which indicates this is only a two-story building. You don't usually need an elevator in a two-story building."

"This is why," Pippa said. She opened a recessed door across the corridor from the elevator. Through it was a vast, airy room lined with bookshelves. A few students sat at wooden tables in the center. "The back entrance to the college library," Pippa explained. "That elevator would help the librarian haul books up and down."

With a jolt of gears, the elevator behind them began to hum. Nancy jumped slightly, startled. A red arrow lit up over the door, indicating that someone was riding up from the ground floor. Silencing Pippa with a quick glance, Nancy flattened herself against the wall perpendicular to the library door. Pippa followed her lead at once.

Nancy peered cautiously around the corner, waiting to see who would step out of the elevator.

The elevator car ground to a halt, and the steel door rolled open. Mr. Sunderwirth stepped off. Though he was dressed more casually than he had been the night before—blue jeans and a plain white shirt—Nancy couldn't mistake that tall, lanky, bespectacled figure for anyone else.

He was carrying a small pile of books and papers under his arm. Nancy's first guess was that he was bound for the library. But after a quick look around, he headed down the corridor—straight for the minstrel's gallery.

Nancy held her breath. Waving to Pippa to stay out of sight, she leaned forward to watch him.

As Mr. Sunderwirth neared the door to the gallery, it opened suddenly. Bess popped her head through, calling out, "No roses, Nancy!" Nearly colliding with him, she let out a startled yelp.

Mr. Sunderwirth stumbled backward as George, too, came barging through the door. The books and papers he had been carrying spilled all over the floor. "Oh, my goodness!" he exclaimed. "What's all this?" In a suspicious tone, he added, "What were you looking for in *there?*"

"Oh, uh, just sightseeing," Bess said.

"You're not members of the college," Mr. Sunderwirth said, leveling a stern gaze at them. "Boniface is off limits to the public until one P.M."

"Oh, they're with me, Mr. Sunderwirth," Pippa called out from behind Nancy, stepping out into the corridor. Nancy followed her.

"Is that Pippa Shaw?" Mr. Sunderwirth asked, squinting through his glasses. "And Nancy Drew?"

"Nice to see you again, Mr. Sunderwirth," Nancy said. "I don't think you've met my friends, Bess Marvin and George Fayne."

"No, I haven't," Mr. Sunderwirth said. He seemed a bit agitated. Squatting down, he hastily began scooping up his scattered belongings.

"Here, let us give you a hand," Bess said. She and George bent over to help him gather up his things. Nancy and Pippa walked down the hall to join them.

Nancy saw Bess pounce on a square buff-colored envelope lying near one wall. As Bess read the outside, her eyes widened. Nancy hurried to her side and glanced at the letter.

On the envelope were three words, handwritten in block letters: "To Miss Innes." And below them was an ugly, menacing drawing of a skull and crossbones.

5

Snatched Away

"You give that back now," Mr. Sunderwirth said sharply, snatching the letter out of Bess's hands. "It's not polite to read other people's mail."

"Sorry," Bess said. She gave him an innocent-looking smile.

He stuffed the envelope hurriedly inside a thick book. "Enjoy your sightseeing," he said. Turning abruptly away from the minstrel's gallery, he strode back down the corridor and went down the stairs.

"He sure acted as if he was hiding something," George said after Mr. Sunderwirth was gone.

"And he sure didn't like us seeing that letter to Miss Innes," Bess added as the four friends began to stroll down the corridor.

"There are plenty of reasons why one don would write a letter to another," Nancy said. "But why

43

put a scary drawing like that on the outside of the envelope? It almost looked like a threat."

They started down the stairs. "Whyever would Mr. Sunderwirth threaten Miss Innes?" Pippa said.

"I don't know," Nancy said, "but we'd better keep an eye on him. Something fishy's going on."

"He was clearly heading to the minstrel's gallery until he saw us," George said.

Nancy frowned, thinking. "Suppose he knew the arrow really was shot at him—not at me or at Miss Innes's empty place. Maybe that's why he wanted to check out the gallery today."

At the bottom of the stairs, a pair of heavy wooden doors led out into a small paved courtyard. "But you said Mr. Sunderwirth dismissed the whole incident as a student prank," Pippa reminded Nancy as they stepped outside.

"True," Nancy said. "And he never even looked at the message written on the other side of the flyer. Still, he might have been only pretending."

"Pippa!" they heard a voice call out. The four young women turned to see Tony D'Souza entering the courtyard. He jogged over to them.

"Did you finish your paper?" Pippa asked him.

Tony rolled his eyes. "I still haven't got a decent conclusion," he said. "It's hopeless. My tutorial's not till four o'clock, but I'm due at my part-time job in the university library at noon. I'm here on scholarship, you see."

"We'll walk over there with you," Nancy said.

"I'd like to see the library anyway. I hear it's one of the best in the world."

"It certainly is," Tony said enthusiastically as he led the way out of the college, through a back gate. "The Bodleian Library holds several million volumes. A copy of every book that's published in Britain is sent here, and the collection of rare old books is incredible."

"I wonder if any of them have black roses in them," Pippa said, half to herself.

"Black roses?" Tony asked.

Tony's immediate interest made Nancy nervous. She didn't entirely trust him, even if he was Pippa's old gymnastics buddy. She nudged Pippa in the back, signaling her to keep quiet.

Pippa stuttered slightly as she covered up. "We're, uh, having a contest to see who can find the most black roses in Oxford." Behind Tony's back, Bess made a face at Nancy. Nancy had to agree that Pippa's excuse was pretty lame.

Tony seemed to buy it, though. "A contest?" he said. "Perhaps I could help you. I love stuff like that—it sounds like something the Puzzlers would have done." He turned into an arched gateway. "Here's the library—these buildings on both sides, plus that round domed building up ahead."

"What section do you work in?" Bess asked.

"Manuscripts," Tony answered, stopping in a small cobbled courtyard. "That's most interesting to me as a historian. The university recently inherited a trunk full of old manuscripts from a Lord Wycherly, and I'm helping to catalog them. I have to do a brief write-up about each document. Most of them are worthless—family letters and land deeds—but I'm hoping I'll come across something valuable. Would you like to come up and see?"

Nancy searched for an excuse, but Pippa was already saying, "Super! Of course we shall."

"This way," Tony said, leading them into a small entryway. They passed up a set of stone stairs. A wooden door on the first landing opened into a bare office, with only a pair of wooden tables and some metal shelves. A brown leather trunk stood open on the floor between the tables.

Tony reached in the trunk and pulled out a thin old book, bound in dusty black leather. "Wycherly Document Number One-oh-two," he said, dropping it on one of the tables. He flipped open a small ledger and made a notation in one column.

Curious, Nancy opened the book. The stiff yellow pages were covered in meticulous black script, written by hand. Incredibly tiny, detailed pictures decorated the margins.

Standing behind Nancy, Tony looked over her shoulder. He let out a low whistle of awe. "In the days before printing presses, some monk must have spent years copying and decorating this text," Tony said. "He didn't just want to copy the words—he wanted to make it beautiful, as a service to God."

Nancy idly turned the page. Her heart skipped a

beat. On the left-hand border, a cascade of tiny black roses tumbled down the edge of the text.

"George, Bess—look at this," Nancy said. She tried not to sound too excited. She didn't want to let Tony think that their search for the rose was anything too important.

But Bess let out a telltale cry of delight. "A black rose! Quick, Nancy, what's behind it?"

Nancy turned the page again. The parchment paper was so thin, she could almost see through it. But the back side of the black rose drawing held nothing special, only more writing.

"Not just one, but a whole bouquet of black roses," Tony said. "You'll win the contest, Nancy."

Nancy carefully leafed through the pages one by one. "Does anybody else work on this project with you?" Nancy asked Tony, trying to sound casual.

He shook his head. "Only my boss, Ms. Jamison, but she hasn't touched the Wycherly papers. I'm supposed to sort through the whole lot by myself. We didn't expect to find anything significant in this trunk—nothing like this."

"Is it really valuable?" Pippa asked.

Tony pursed his lips. "Well, perhaps not as valuable as the illuminated manuscripts across town in the Ashmolean Museum. They're more richly illustrated, with much more gold lettering. This one's not nearly so precious—at least, not as an art object. But maybe it's an important social document."

Nancy perked up. Could the manuscript contain information about the riddle's "grievous crime"? "What does it say?" she asked Tony.

He squinted at the squiggly letters. "I'm afraid it's in French, and my French is dismal. But from what I can read, I think it's an instruction manual for novice monks."

"Where did the trunk come from?" George asked.

Tony looked vague. "Lord Wycherly died about a year ago," he said. "He willed these documents to the university. When his relatives cleaned out his mansion, they threw everything into this trunk. It was delivered to us from his solicitor's office."

"A solicitor is what we call a lawyer," Pippa explained to the Americans.

Tony crooked an eyebrow. "Why so curious?" he asked. "I thought you were just having fun spotting black roses around town."

"Oh, we're interested in all kinds of old stuff," Nancy said in an offhand tone.

"Well, I'm going to ask Ms. Jamison if I can take this book to Miss Innes," Tony decided, taking the book from Nancy and snapping it shut. "She'll be able to look it over and tell me what we've got."

"Mind if we go with you?" Nancy asked.

"Of course, if you want to," Tony said, but he sounded uncertain. "Only it's a lot of fuss over a book that may be worthless."

Tony wrapped up the book in a brown paper bag for protection. As the five of them left the room, he locked the door behind them. They stopped by Ms. Jamison's office, on the ground floor, to get her permission to take the manuscript to Miss Innes. Then they headed for Boniface.

"Perhaps this will make up for my not finishing the paper," Tony said, making a nervous joke as they cut across the main quadrangle.

On the far side of the quadrangle, they went up a short set of steps and through a covered passageway to a heavy oak door. Tony knocked.

The door buzzed and swung open automatically. Nancy and her friends hung back in the hall as Tony paused in the doorway.

Dorothy Innes sat in her wheelchair beside a graceful white writing desk. Her sitting room was beautifully decorated, with pale blue carpeting, plump blue velvet sofas, and two walls filled with books. A large window with small leaded panes looked out on the main college garden.

Miss Innes looked surprised to see Tony. "Mr. D'Souza," she called out. "A bit early, aren't you?"

"Pardon me for barging in like this," Tony said. "But I need to ask you about something— something besides medieval land reform."

Miss Innes smiled. "Oh, good. Even medieval land reform can get boring when you've taught it as many years as I have."

Looking past Tony, she noticed the four young women. "Oh, permit me to introduce my friends," Tony said. "This is Pippa Shaw—her father's Derek Shaw, the law professor—"

"I know Miss Shaw," Miss Innes said. "And I believe I have met her three American friends."

"Yes, we met you in the Senior Common Room last night," Nancy said, moving into the room.

Miss Innes shifted uneasily and darted a quick glance over her shoulder, looking out the window behind her. As she twisted in her chair, Nancy noticed a black enamel brooch on her shoulder—a brooch in the shape of a rose.

Surprised, Nancy blurted out, "Your brooch—"

Miss Innes stared down to check which pin she was wearing. Nancy thought she detected a flush on the elderly don's cheek. "What about my brooch?" she asked, flustered. "It was a gift from . . . a friend. Gwyneth Davies, in fact, if you must know." She cleared her throat brusquely. "Well, Mr. D'Souza, what did you come to ask me about?"

Tony laid the manuscript on her desk. After unwrapping it, he opened it to the first page. He explained where the manuscript had come from. "I hoped you could tell me if it's valuable."

"Let me see," she said, studying the page gravely. "This is in medieval French, you know. I can't make it all out. . . ."

Nancy watched Miss Innes closely as she turned the page and saw the painted black roses. The woman's keen, wrinkled face was as still as a mask.

"Maybe one of the French dons could translate it for us," Tony said. "Mr. Sunderwirth, perhaps."

"No! Not Sunderwirth." Miss Innes's blue-veined hands gripped the book. "I'll keep it here with me."

Tony looked uncertain. "But it's library property," he began. "Ms. Jamison didn't say anything about leaving it here."

"I'll call your Miss Jamison and set it right with her," Miss Innes said, suddenly stern. "Now, you get back to the library. I'll see you again at four o'clock." After placing the book in her lap, Miss Innes reached back and wheeled her chair toward the door. The five young people had no choice but to file out of her apartment.

Tony headed back to work, while Nancy and her friends decided to eat lunch. Pippa invited them to her home, just across the Cherwell River from Boniface. On the way, they chatted about their visit with Miss Innes.

"She did seem distracted, just as Tony described," Bess said. "But she was pretty fierce about not letting go of that manuscript."

"I wonder if it's because the manuscript is so valuable, or because she's looking for black roses, too," Nancy said. "Or is it just because she doesn't trust Mr. Sunderwirth?"

"Speaking of not trusting someone, Nancy, why won't you let me tell Tony why we're looking for black roses?" Pippa asked as they turned into the Shaws' tidy front garden. She took out her door key. "He's an awfully decent bloke, you know."

Before Nancy could answer, they heard a telephone ringing from inside the house. "I hate it when the phone rings just as I'm unlocking the door," Pippa declared.

The lock clicked, and Pippa shoved open the door. She dashed in and ran for the telephone, on a low table in the front hall. "Hello?" she said breathlessly as she picked up the receiver.

Nancy followed Pippa inside. She glanced around the neat, comfortable-looking house, then looked up at Pippa, who was silently listening to the caller.

Pippa had turned pale, and she clenched the phone to her ear so tightly that her knuckles turned white. "Pippa?" Nancy asked.

Pippa's arm dropped, and she hung up with a clatter. She turned to Nancy, tears filling her eyes.

"He said . . . he said I'd better stop snooping around—if I want to stay alive."

6

A Dangerous Dead End

Nancy put her arm around Pippa's shoulders. "Start from the beginning," she gently told her friend. "What did the caller say exactly?"

Pippa took a deep breath. "When I answered, he said, 'Pippa?' I said yes," she recalled. She shut her eyes tightly to focus her memory. "Then he said, 'Listen clearly: You'd better stop snooping around if you want to stay alive.' And then he hung up."

Nancy exchanged glances with George and Bess. "Was it a voice you recognized?" she asked. Pippa shook her head. "Can you describe it to me?"

"It sounded as though he was trying to disguise his voice," Pippa said. "With a sort of a growl in his throat. But he didn't have a really deep voice. I think it was a young person rather than an old one."

"And you're sure it was a man?" Nancy asked.

Pippa nodded. "Sorry to be so feeble," she said in a shaky voice, "but . . . well, it's not every day I receive a death threat."

"Nancy gets them all the time, don't you, Nan?" Bess said, trying to cheer up Pippa.

Nancy smiled. "We should still take it seriously," she said. "Even if this anonymous caller doesn't really intend to hurt you, Pippa, which he probably doesn't. It's usually just a bluff."

Nancy suggested that they all go sit down in the kitchen, where they helped themselves to sandwiches and milk. Pippa put a kettle on to make some tea.

"One thing about the anonymous call—it does tell us that somebody else knows we're looking for something," George said after they'd sat down at the kitchen table. "Who's seen us 'snooping'?"

"Mr. Cole saw us in the dining hall last night, looking at the carved crest," Bess said. "Mr. Austin knew what we were doing, too."

"Mr. Cole would never make a threatening call," Pippa said, putting down her sandwich and looking horrified. "He's a very distinguished scholar. And Mr. Austin's always been so sweet to me, ever since I was a little girl."

"Mr. Sunderwirth saw us coming out of the minstrel's gallery," George said, checking off suspects on her fingers. "Tony D'Souza knows we're looking for a black rose. And Miss Innes knows that we know about the manuscript Tony found."

Nancy thoughtfully took a sip of cold milk.

Setting down her glass, she said, "That's an awful lot of suspects. But at this point, we can't rule out anybody. This threatening call does tell us one thing—that the message on the arrow was no mere prank. Somebody shot that arrow, trying to get us to find something. And someone else sure doesn't want us to find it."

"But, Dad, I can't give up on the case now!" Nancy told her father. As they had arranged, she had met him on the steps of the law library at two-thirty, just to touch base. George had stayed with her, while Pippa and Bess had gone to the Ashmolean Museum to hunt for black roses.

Carson Drew sighed. "It's not my decision, it's Mr. Cole's," he told her. "He won't let you pry up the paneling in the dining hall. He won't give you keys so you can search around Boniface. He just doesn't think there's a real case here."

"Did you show him the note attached to the arrow?" George asked.

Mr. Drew pulled the folded flyer out of his pocket and handed it back to Nancy. "Yes," he said. "He still thinks it's just a prank. I did ask him if he recognized the handwriting. He said no."

"But it isn't just the arrow anymore, Dad," Nancy said. "We saw that young French don, Mr. Sunderwirth, poking around the minstrel's gallery, and he was carrying a threatening-looking letter addressed to Miss Innes. What if the arrow is part of a scheme to harass her or blackmail her?"

55

"I hate to think of that fine old woman in trouble," Mr. Drew said, frowning. "Do you have any other evidence of harassment?"

"Well, nothing except her manner," Nancy said. "Apparently she's been jumpy and moody lately. But get this, Dad. Pippa got a threatening phone call this afternoon, too. An anonymous caller told her to stop snooping around."

Mr. Drew looked startled and concerned. "I don't like the sound of that," he said.

"Maybe if you told Mr. Cole about the threat, he'd start cooperating," George said.

Mr. Drew sighed. "Okay, I'll try him again. And I'll ask him for a little background on Miss Innes's situation, as well as on this Sunderwirth fellow."

"But one thing, Dad." Nancy paused to choose her words carefully. "Don't tell the master too much. I can't help thinking . . . well, isn't it weird that he's been trying to block our investigation all along? He's one of the few people who knows for certain what we're looking for, and why. What if *he's* the one who made that call to Pippa?"

"I can't imagine how he could be involved," Mr. Drew argued. "We're talking about a prominent man here. And he has a good reason for refusing to let you take apart that carved paneling."

"I realize that, Dad," Nancy said. "Anyhow, who knows whether the black rose in the paneling is the one we want? We saw another black rose in a medieval manuscript this morning, and we're looking for others. All I'm saying is that our job would

56

be a lot easier if Mr. Cole gave us the run of the college. I hate having to sneak around."

"Mr. Cole did have one suggestion," Mr. Drew said.

"What is it?" Nancy asked hopefully.

"Since the riddle was written on the back of a flyer for a play," he said, "maybe you should read the play. The riddle might be a quote from it."

Nancy flashed him a discouraged look. "We'll check it out. But that's just typical of Mr. Cole. He still thinks the arrow's message was just a publicity stunt for the play."

"Did you tell Mr. Cole how much experience Nancy has in this sort of thing?" George asked Mr. Drew. "You know, a lot of people don't take us seriously because we're so young."

"Maybe that would persuade him," Mr. Drew said. "As I said, I'll speak with the man again. But with these threats and all, I want you to be careful. I know you've dealt with plenty of danger in the past, Nancy, but there's no sense looking for trouble."

After making plans to meet for dinner, Mr. Drew returned to his library research, and Nancy and George went to meet Bess and Pippa. As soon as she saw them coming out the front door of the museum, Nancy could tell they'd had no luck. "Would you believe it? We couldn't spot a single black rose in the place," Bess declared.

"Lots of red and white roses, but no blacks," Pippa added. "Though I have to admit, my head's positively swimming from looking at so many objects. We could have missed it."

"So what do we do next?" Bess asked Nancy.

"I guess we should start searching for the rose, through all thirty colleges," Nancy said as they strolled back toward Boniface. "Only let's not divide up the work four ways. After that threat, Pippa, I think we ought to stay in teams."

"Sounds like a good idea to me," Pippa said, looking relieved.

Nancy looked up at the front window of a bookstore they were passing. "Oh, that reminds me, let's get a copy of *Tragedie of the Black Knight*. Mr. Cole suggested to my dad that the riddle might be a quote from the play. We should check it out."

"The play!" Pippa said, smacking her forehead. "I completely forgot to get tickets for us for tomorrow night. I'd better do it now."

"I'll come with you," George said.

Agreeing to meet at four o'clock at the tea shop Pippa recommended, the four girls split up. Bess and Nancy headed into the bookstore. "There's the drama section, over there," Bess said, pointing toward the back of the shop. She barged ahead.

But Nancy halted. She had just noticed Mr. Sunderwirth, browsing at the shelves nearest the door. Looking up, he noticed her, too. To her surprise, he gave her a friendly smile.

"So we meet again," he said. "I'm glad I ran into you. I don't know where my head was when I saw you earlier." He took a step toward Nancy.

58

Nancy's suspicions sharpened. "You did seem a little flustered," she said warily.

"I meant to tell you, have you seen *The Monkey Puzzle* yet?" he said.

Surprised at the change in subject, Nancy stammered. "W-well, no . . ."

"Because if you haven't, you can get tickets right here in Oxford," he told her. "There's a ticket agency on the High Street, Juliet Brian. I walked by there this morning, and an ad in the front window said they've still got *Monkey Puzzle* seats for the weekend. I thought of you straight off."

"That's very nice of you," Nancy said. "I'll have to go check that out."

Bess came up behind Nancy. "Found it," she said, waving a paperback copy of *Tragedie of the Black Knight*. Seeing Mr. Sunderwirth, she looked taken aback.

"We're going to the college play tomorrow night," Nancy explained to him while Bess went to pay for the book. "We thought we should read the script beforehand."

"I think you'll find it's not much of a play," he said. "The Black Knight gets all the good lines. But no doubt Coningsby will do a bang-up job."

Oddly, Mr. Sunderwirth stuck with them as they left the bookstore. *Is he tailing us for some reason?* Nancy wondered to herself. In the street outside, she turned to him and pointedly said, "Well, we're going the other way. Goodbye."

"Don't forget the ticket agent," Mr. Sunderwirth

said, pushing his glasses up on his nose. "There's actually a shortcut to the High Street from here. Would you like directions?"

Nancy was beginning to get impatient. "Sure, okay," she said.

With precise hand gestures, he launched into describing a detailed route through back streets and alleys. Nancy and Bess listened with growing confusion. "You can't get lost," he said at the end.

"I'm sure we won't," Nancy said. "Thanks. 'Bye."

Nancy and Bess walked off briskly in the direction he had indicated. "He's still watching us," Bess said, stealing a glance over her shoulder.

"Then we'd better take the route he told us," Nancy said. Ahead, she spotted a narrow opening in the wall on their right. "That must be the alley he was talking about."

They turned in. The alley took a couple of abrupt twists, leading them deeper and deeper into a maze of stone walls. "Are you sure this leads somewhere?" Bess asked in a nervous voice.

"Shh," Nancy hushed her. Listening intently, she thought she heard footsteps behind them. "Don't look now, but I think someone's following us."

Pulling Bess by the arm, Nancy hurried forward. The lane took another right angle, and they found themselves facing a tiny pub, squeezed between the walls. With its half-timbered walls of white plaster and black beams, it was a picturesque sight.

"There's the way out, Nan," Bess said, pointing to another narrow lane beside the pub. The girls jogged along it, emerging onto a wider street. "Maybe the person behind us was just heading for the pub," Bess suggested.

Nancy flattened herself against the nearest wall. "There's one way to find out," she said.

A blue-jeaned leg began to step out of the lane to the pub—and immediately drew back.

"Let's go!" Nancy whispered. The two young women darted back into the lane. They could hear running footsteps echo off the walls ahead of them.

As they passed the pub again, Nancy spotted a shadow darting down the other lane. She shifted into high gear, plunging into the twisting back alley.

Nancy lurched around a turn and halted. A small wooden door was set in the wall. She hadn't noticed it before. Could their pursuer have gone in there?

As she hesitated, she heard a scraping sound above her head. She looked upward, just as Bess reeled around the corner, clutching her book in her hand.

Bess let out a scream. "Nancy—look out!"

A chunk of stone toppled off the wall—right toward Nancy.

7

Things Get Nasty

The stone block hurtled toward the pavement. As it crashed against one wall and then the other, it ripped a metal street lamp right out of its bracket.

Nancy crouched low, arms tucked tightly over her head. Chips of stone rained on her shoulders.

The block came to rest only a few inches from Nancy. Hearing it land, she raised her head.

"Nancy—are you okay?" Bess cried out. She ran over to Nancy, who was dusting fragments of stone from her hair and T-shirt.

"All in one piece," she reported grimly. "But I'll tell you one thing, Bess, that was no accident. Look at this stone."

Bess touched the stone block. "What about it?"

"Look at the color," Nancy pointed out. "It's the same golden color as the buildings in Boniface. But these walls are made of gray stone."

Bess looked up and around. "And their surface is rougher," she said. "You're right, Nan. This stone didn't simply fall off that wall. Do you think the person who was chasing us pushed it over?"

"I'd bet money on it," Nancy replied. "And I think I know how he did it."

Nancy scrambled to her feet and leaped over to the wooden doorway. She tried the handle, but the door wouldn't budge.

"Come on, Bess," Nancy said. "We've got to find out what's on the other side of this wall. And if we hurry, we may find *who's* on the other side, too."

Setting off at a run, Nancy and Bess followed the lane back to the street. Nancy's sense of direction told her to turn right and follow the gray stone wall. Several yards down was an arched gateway, with massive wooden doors standing open.

"It looks like an old castle," Bess said.

"We're lucky no one pulled up the drawbridge," Nancy said, making a wry joke.

They turned through the gateway and raced into the open courtyard beyond. "Hey!" a porter called out from the gate lodge. Nancy and Bess pulled to a halt. "You're not members of college. Twenty-five pence entrance fee," he growled.

"Please, we're not just sightseeing," Nancy said, trying to catch her breath. "Someone just threw a rock over the wall at us."

The porter raised his bushy gray eyebrows. "Threw a rock, you say?"

"Not just a rock—a boulder!" Bess exclaimed.

Between her book and her other hand, she demonstrated the size of it.

"We were in that lane that leads to the pub," Nancy explained. "A piece of stone nearly fell on us—and not the same kind of stone as the wall."

"I don't like the sound of that," the porter said. "Folks can't do that sort of thing in *my* college. Wait a sec." He ducked inside for a moment, then stepped out carrying a jangling ring of keys.

Striding beside him, Nancy and Bess followed the wall. A low college building abutted it there. Where the wall took a right angle, the building did, too. "The lane runs just the other side of the wall," the porter said. "It turns the corner there."

They turned and followed the wall for several yards. "How far along do you reckon you were?" the porter asked Nancy.

"Farther than this, I'm sure," she said.

They skirted a wing of the low building where it jutted away from the wall. After passing through an archway, they entered another small quadrangle. Nancy pointed excitedly across the quad. "There—that's the stone!" she said.

A heap of rubble was piled by the gray outer wall. Several chunks of golden stone lay on top.

"That's left over from some renovation," the porter said. "We've made some small repairs in our college chapel, and we're knocking down a wall of the library to add some faculty offices. Our library was built in the eighteenth century, with different stone from the rest of St. Cyril's."

Nancy sprinted over to the rubble. Next to it, a high grassy bank ran halfway up the wall. "What's this?" she asked the porter.

"Part of the original city walls," he explained. "St. Cyril's is one of Oxford's oldest colleges, you know. The walls fell down from age, back in the seventeenth century. We left the ruins here, and the grass has grown over it."

Nancy sized up the scene. Someone tall could have climbed up the overgrown ruins and reached the top of the wall. She examined the ground, but neither the paving stones nor the grassy bank showed any trace of footprints.

"Why, if it isn't—Bess, right?" Simon Coningsby's resonant voice interrupted Nancy's thoughts. She turned to see him sauntering across the quad. The faded denim of his jacket and jeans perfectly matched the trace of blue in his gray eyes. "What are you doing in St. Cyril's?"

Before Bess could answer, the porter said, "Someone pitched a block of stone over the wall— nearly cracked the girls' heads open."

Simon's handsome face grimaced in concern. "That's horrible! Did you see who it was?"

Spurred by Simon's sympathy, Bess trembled with a delayed reaction of fear. "We ran around as fast as we could to try to catch him," she said.

"I didn't see anyone suspicious coming out the gate," the porter said.

"But what about the back entrance?" Simon said. Nancy instantly remembered the wooden door they'd seen in the wall. That must have been how their pursuer had slipped inside St. Cyril's.

The porter knit his eyebrows. "It's locked."

"Oh, students are always leaving it unlocked," Simon said, "so that they can get in and out of college after hours. I do it myself when I'm here visiting friends. Let's check."

He led them to the adjacent building and through an open entryway. Nancy saw the wood door on a back wall. A broom had been propped under the handle, wedging it shut. When Simon removed the broom, the handle turned, and the door opened.

"It was unlocked, all right," he said. "But someone jammed it shut with this broom. Probably didn't want you coming in after him."

"So it was someone who knows his way around this college," Bess said.

"Well, there are about three hundred students in St. Cyril's," Simon said. "Plus all the members of other colleges who come regularly to visit friends or take a tutorial with St. Cyril's dons. That narrows it down to about a thousand suspects."

Nancy sighed. "And while we were here, our culprit probably walked out the front gate."

"I'm sorry we didn't catch the blighter," the porter said. "But now, if you're all right, I should be getting back to the lodge."

"Thanks for your help, Mr. Godwin," Simon said. "I'll show the girls out."

Mr. Godwin trudged out of the back quad. "I'm

just glad you two weren't hurt," Simon said to Nancy and Bess. "It's dangerous to prowl around back streets, you know."

Bess hugged her play book to her chest and gave Simon a starry-eyed look. "Maybe we'd be safer if *you* had time to show us around."

He laughed lightly. "Wish I could, Bess. But I've got a tutorial in about ten minutes. I can show you St. Cyril's chapel, though. Each college has its own chapel, but St. Cyril's may be the finest."

Simon led them back into the front courtyard. Across from the main gates stood a small stone church, with arched stained-glass windows and bronze doors. Simon, Nancy, and Bess walked up the steps and into the cool, dark interior.

"Whoa! Get a load of that," Bess said. She and Nancy both stared at the huge, round stained-glass window at the far end of the chapel. Sunlight filtered through the dark purplish windows, outlined by black lead frames.

"That's the famous rose window," Simon said.

"Did you say *rose* window?" Bess asked. She and Nancy traded glances.

"Why, yes—it's a fairly common church feature," Simon said. "The symmetrical pattern is supposed to resemble a rose."

"It looks like a black rose, Nancy," Bess said softly.

"But there's nothing 'behind' it but sky," Nancy said. "Not even a tower of another building."

"Why should something be behind it?" Simon asked.

"Oh, no reason," Nancy told him. "But I was wondering, what's on the other side of this wall?"

Simon looked baffled. "I have no idea. We can walk outside and look, I guess."

The three of them trotted out and circled the chapel. On the other side of the altar wall lay a broad lawn with a surface as smooth and even as velvet. Nancy scratched her head. "Nothing could have been buried here," she said with a sigh.

"There's an old Oxford joke about that," Simon said. "Someone asks an Oxford college gardener how he makes the lawns so smooth, and he answers, 'You plant grass seed, you water it, and you cut it. And then you leave it alone for six centuries.'"

Nancy smiled. "I'm sure no one's disturbed this ground for at least that long," she said. "Well, thanks for showing us around, Simon. We don't want to make you late for your tutorial."

He checked his watch. "I'd better go. See you—cheers!" He sprinted off across the lawn.

"I have absolutely never met anyone so adorable," Bess said to Nancy with a sigh.

"Yeah, yeah, I've heard that before," Nancy said, grinning. "Come on, Bess, let's go."

After leaving St. Cyril's, Nancy and Bess strolled to Boniface Lane, a street near Boniface's front gate. Pippa and George were waiting for them outside the Devon Tea Shop, a quaint half-timbered restaurant. They went inside and sat in a bow window overlooking the lane. Pippa ordered cream teas—pots of tea accompanied by flaky scones topped with strawberry jam and thick, rich Devonshire cream.

Bess laid her book on the table and took a bite. "This is divine!" she exclaimed. "And I bet it has about a million calories in it."

"A million and two," Pippa said. "But every one is worth it." She licked her fingers.

"So how was your afternoon?" George asked Nancy and Bess. "Did you make any progress on the case?"

"Well, someone is still trying to stop our investigation," Nancy said. She described her near miss with the falling block of stone. "The only clue we have is that our pursuer was wearing blue jeans. I do recall that Mr. Sunderwirth was wearing jeans today. And he *was* the one who told us to go down that back-alley route in the first place."

"But, Nancy, this is a college town," George said. "I'll bet half the population of Oxford at any given moment is wearing blue jeans."

Pippa's eyes grew wide. "Nancy, this is becoming awfully dangerous. First the phone threat, now this. Maybe we ought to quit."

"You said you wanted to help us solve a mystery," Bess said. "Well, this sort of stuff happens when you solve mysteries."

"Things do seem to be heating up," Nancy said.

69

"But we're still far from narrowing down our hunt for the black rose." She told Pippa and George about the rose window in St. Cyril's chapel.

"The rose window may be a red herring," Bess said, "but who cares, with Simon Coningsby there to show us around. That reminds me, did you get the tickets for the play?"

"Yep," George said. "Tomorrow night, seven o'clock." She looked out the window and paused, frowning. "There's Tony—but he's not going into the college, he's running out. And he looks upset."

Nancy twisted in her seat to see Tony D'Souza stagger to a stop outside, looking confused. She jumped to her feet and ran out of the tea shop.

"Nancy!" Tony shouted, and waved his arm. They ran to meet each other. "You're just the person I was hoping to find," he said, panting.

"What is it, Tony?" Nancy asked with concern.

"I've just come from my tutorial with Miss Innes," he replied. "The police were there. A thief broke into her study and tried to steal the Wycherly manuscript!"

8

The Searchers

Nancy gripped Tony's shoulder. "Did the thief take the manuscript from Miss Innes?" she asked.

He shook his head. "It's still there," he said. "But she's pretty rattled by the whole episode."

"I'd like to go see her," Nancy said quickly. "Pippa and George and Bess are over there having tea—"

"In the Devon?" Tony said. "I'll go tell them where you've gone, and I'll catch up with you."

"Thanks," Nancy said, grateful for Tony's swift thinking. She spun around, jogged through the main gate, and crossed the quadrangle to Miss Innes's apartment.

The door was standing ajar. Hesitantly, Nancy nudged it open and stepped into the doorway.

Miss Innes was sitting in her wheelchair beside the desk, bent over with her head in her hands. A

71

middle-aged man in a gray tweed jacket stood awkwardly beside her, a small notebook open in his hand. Nancy guessed at once that he was a police detective. A young man—probably his assistant, Nancy thought—was busy examining the window, where several panes had been smashed in.

The detective flashed Nancy a challenging stare. "Uh—Miss Innes, you have a visitor," he said. Miss Innes looked up.

Nancy braced herself for Miss Innes's disapproval. Instead, to her surprise, the don breathed a sigh of relief. "Did Tony tell you what happened?" she asked.

Nancy nodded. "I hope you're all right."

"I'd gone over to the Senior Common Room to get a quick cup of tea," Miss Innes said in a shaky voice. "I came back right before four o'clock. As soon as I entered the room, I saw that my window had been broken open. The thief had scattered a few things around, but the apartment wasn't ransacked or anything. Inspector Morris thinks that indicates that the thief soon found what he was looking for."

"Now, Miss Innes, there's no point in telling the young lady the whole story," the detective said guardedly.

Miss Innes waved him away impatiently. "Miss Drew was the one who brought me the manuscript," she said in a brusque tone.

"I thought you said it came from a Mr. D'Souza,"

Morris said, checking his notebook. "On loan from the university library."

"They brought it here together," Miss Innes said. "I must tell her what happened. As I was saying, Miss Drew, I'd left the book on my desk, in plain sight. It seems the thief moved it under a lamp to inspect it, then tossed it onto the floor. He went out through the door, apparently. It was unlatched when I returned. Nothing else is missing."

"As far as we know," Inspector Morris pointed out. "Now, Miss Innes—"

"Have you finished dusting the book for fingerprints?" Miss Innes demanded.

The younger detective spoke up. "Yes, ma'am. But I couldn't get any useful prints. The book has been handled by too many people lately."

"Then you won't be needing it for evidence?" she asked.

Inspector Morris shook his head. "Not as far as I can see," he said. "Since nothing has been stolen, all we've got here is a simple case of breaking and entering. And frankly, I can't imagine we'll ever find the culprit."

"I know what you're really saying—this case is not important, so you won't bother to find the culprit," Miss Innes said tartly.

Tony appeared in the doorway. "Everything all right?" he asked anxiously.

Miss Innes reached over to her desk and grasped the manuscript. "Here, Tony," she said, thrusting it into his hands. "You take this back to the library, where it'll be safe. I don't want to worry about a repeat visit from that burglar."

"Did you have a chance to look it over?" Tony asked, his voice rising eagerly. "Is it really valuable after all?"

"Not very," she answered with a shrug. "There are several existing manuscripts of this particular instruction book. I thought this one might have something special"—her gaze flickered to Nancy for a second—"but it didn't."

"Inspector Morris?" Nancy asked. "If you've finished investigating the crime scene, may I take a look around myself?"

He frowned. "I'm not sure we are finished," he began.

"Oh, let her poke around, for goodness' sake," Miss Innes broke in. "The girl's an experienced detective, from the States."

"You are?" Tony asked Nancy, looking surprised.

Nancy flushed and nodded. It seemed there was no way she could prevent Tony from learning about her investigation.

"Besides, her father's a friend of Derek Shaw's," Miss Innes said. "You know Derek Shaw. I believe he's been helpful to the Oxford police a few times."

Inspector Morris heaved a sigh. "All right, Miss Drew. Inspector Corbin, Miss Drew can help you search the room for clues."

The younger detective gave her a friendly nod.

Miss Innes took hold of her wheels. "Well, then, I suppose we can go now, Inspector," she announced. "I'll show you around the college so you can get an idea of its layout. By the way, Mr. D'Souza, you needn't come back after you take that book to the library. I know you never finished your paper for today." She threw him a withering look.

Miss Innes trundled away with the senior detective, and Tony left carrying the manuscript. Nancy was left with Inspector Corbin. "Now I know what they mean by the phrase 'eccentric professor,'" he said, jerking his head in the direction Miss Innes had just gone. "Say, you let me know if you find any clues, all right?"

"Will do," Nancy said.

First she inspected the window. A few small panes had been broken, making an opening just large enough to reach in and unlatch the window from within. She could see the fragments of shattered glass on the pale blue carpet. That proved the glass had been broken from the outside. Leaning out the window, she looked down to see that the flower bed below had been lightly trampled. There were no clear footprints, however.

Next she checked the carpet for muddy footprints, but there were none. Moving over to the desk, she carefully looked it over. A few papers were scattered about—students' papers and photocopied college notices. A paperweight lay toppled on its side, a small alabaster figure of a Greek goddess aiming a bow and arrow at a deer.

She studied the shelves beside the desk. There, in an ebony picture frame, was a black-and-white photo of a half-dozen dons in black robes. Smiling and holding goblets high, they appeared to be toasting the camera. "The Puzzlers," Nancy murmured.

Leaning over, she picked out the two women in the picture. One was familiar to Nancy from many book jackets—the hawk-nosed face of Dame Gwyneth Davies. The other woman was barely recognizable as a much younger Dorothy Innes.

The corner of a buff-colored envelope poked out from behind the picture frame. Was it the letter Mr. Sunderwirth had dropped on the floor that morning? Nancy pulled out the envelope from where it had been stashed away, half hidden, on the shelf.

The handwriting on the front looked the same: "To Miss Innes." And there was the same leering skull and crossbones drawn below it.

Nancy lifted the flap of the envelope, which had been broken open. She pulled out a sheet of plain stationery.

In the same crude block letters, a short message had been written: "You know I can see you. Keep your mouth shut if you want to live."

The nasty message made Nancy shiver. If this was what Mr. Sunderwirth had been sending, no wonder he hadn't wanted Nancy and her friends to see it.

"Say there, I was just thinking," Inspector Corbin called from the other side of the room. Acting on reflex, Nancy slipped the letter in the pocket of her jeans before turning.

"What?" she asked.

"Miss Innes is in a wheelchair, right?" the police officer said. "Isn't it odd that her study is up a flight of steps? I mean, how does she get in and out herself?"

"Good question," Nancy said. "I hadn't thought about it. Let's go outside and see."

Together they walked out the front door of the study, into the covered passageway. There were eight stone steps leading down to the quadrangle— and no ramp. But halfway along the passageway, Nancy spotted a narrow side corridor turning off. She and Inspector Corbin followed it.

The corridor led past a couple of office doors, their brass nameplates bearing dons' names. A stone arch led into a second building, with a short ramp compensating for a slight change in floor level. "They must have installed that especially for Miss Innes," the inspector said.

They followed the corridor around a right turn. "This looks familiar," Nancy said. "I think it's the ground floor of the wing underneath the library. I was here this morning—or at any rate, I was directly upstairs from here." She pushed open the door leading into the small back courtyard. "This must be the entrance Miss Innes uses. It's level with the ground. No steps."

"And there's an elevator she can use if she needs to go up to the next floor," Inspector Corbin said, pointing over to the tiny elevator in the corner.

Nancy nodded. "I expect it was originally installed for the librarians to use, hauling books up and down," she said. "But no doubt it comes in handy for Miss Innes, too. Well, that answers our question."

Nancy and the police inspector retraced their steps back to Miss Innes's apartment. "Must be a bit of a bore for her, going this same twisty route several times a day," he said.

"I have a hard enough time finding my way around Oxford, and I have the use of my legs," Nancy said. "I can't imagine how difficult it is for someone in a wheelchair."

As they turned into the passageway outside Miss Innes's apartment, Nancy came to a startled halt. She saw someone hiding behind a stone pillar at the end of the passageway. Was it the thief, returning to the scene of the crime?

Nancy ducked back in the doorway, but Inspector Corbin marched on. The figure behind the pillar moved quickly, as if to avoid being seen. Nancy spotted a leg—wearing blue jeans. Just like the person who'd followed her through that back alley!

Nancy's mind raced. Could the thief be the same person who had pushed the stone down at her? Her mad chase through the maze of back lanes had taken place around three-fifteen or three-thirty, she estimated. While she and Bess had been inspecting the site at St. Cyril's, the culprit could have run back to Boniface and broken into Miss Innes's apartment. Miss Innes had said she'd returned shortly before four. The time frame was tight, but possible.

Nancy peered around the doorpost again. The figure moved out from behind the pillar, and Nancy gasped.

It was Tony.

"Hi, sir," he said politely to Inspector Corbin. "I came back to see if there was any news."

"Nothing right now—sorry," the officer said.

Nancy realized guiltily that Tony hadn't been hiding at all, only leaning against the pillar. And the fact that he was wearing jeans was almost irrelevant—as George had pointed out, half the people in Oxford wore blue jeans.

"Tony!" she called out, stepping into the passageway. "I thought you weren't coming back after the library."

"It's not out of my way. My room's just on the other side of the Old Quad," Tony said. His face brightened as he saw her. "And I was so eager to learn if you'd found any clues."

Tony shifted his weight anxiously from foot to foot, twisting a signet ring on his left hand. Nancy's eyes fell on Tony's finger.

She stopped and stared at the ring. Its square-cut face looked like shiny black onyx. An image was carved into the surface.

"Tony, don't think I'm crazy, but . . . can I see your ring?" Nancy asked.

With a look of surprise, Tony held out his hand. In the golden late-afternoon light, Nancy peered hard at the image engraved in the black stone.

It was a rose!

9

Black as Night

Nancy tried to keep her voice calm. "Nice ring, Tony," she said. "Where'd it come from?"

"I don't know for certain," Tony admitted. "I've had it since I was a little boy, but I only started wearing it lately. It was too big for my finger before."

Was it just a coincidence that Tony had a black rose on his ring? Nancy wondered. Or was he personally connected to this case in some way?

And if he was, why hadn't he told the girls?

"Did you realize that it's a black rose?" Nancy asked, watching his face for his reaction.

Tony's dark eyes grew startled. "A black rose?" He looked down at his ring. "Why, so it is! I hadn't even noticed. Well, there's another one for your contest."

His surprise seems genuine, Nancy thought. Or is he just a good actor?

"This ring has always meant a great deal to me," Tony said, studying it as he leaned against the pillar. "It came from my mother. She died when I was four."

Nancy's heart stirred. "I'm sorry," she said. "My mother died when I was little, too."

Tony looked up and gave her a sympathetic gaze. "Then you understand," he said. "My father— well, let's simply say he's reserved. He hardly ever talked about Mum after she died. One day I found her jewel case in a drawer. One of the things I found inside was this ring, so I put it on. When my father saw it, he was absolutely furious at first."

"Maybe you stirred up painful memories for him," Nancy said.

"I didn't mean to," Tony said. "All I wanted was to learn about my mother. At any rate, when he calmed down, he said I could keep the ring—that my mother had saved it for me. I assume it came from her family."

"May I see it?" Nancy asked in a casual tone.

"Sure," Tony said. He slid the ring off his finger and handed it to her.

After studying the ring's face, Nancy slid a finger behind it, feeling for a secret compartment. But the gold setting was smooth and solid.

"It's certainly handsome," Nancy said, handing it back. "It must be very special to you. I know I treasure everything I have that came from my mom."

Tony gave her a warm smile. "Can I walk you somewhere? Are you eating dinner here in the hall again tonight?"

"No, we were only invited for yesterday evening," Nancy said.

"Too bad," Tony said. "Last night you got an arrow for dessert. Who knows what you'd get tonight?" With a cheerful wave, he strolled off across the quad.

Nancy watched him go with a puzzled frown. Tony now knew she was a detective, thanks to Miss Innes. And he knew that she and her friends were looking for black roses, though he still didn't know why. How much more should she let him know?

Nancy had a nagging feeling that Tony had a secret. What could it be?

"I'll have the spaghetti with grilled shrimp," Mr. Drew told the waitress at dinner that night.

"And that's one spaghetti carbonara for the friend you're waiting for." She flipped shut her pad, took their menus, and left the table.

"What a great gimmick—a restaurant that serves only spaghetti," Bess said. "Thirty-five different spaghetti dishes. No wonder Pippa says it's such a popular student hangout." She craned her neck to search the big, bright, noisy restaurant. Then she ducked. "Don't look now, guys, but Simon's here."

Nancy looked over Bess's head. The handsome young actor sat two tables away, entertaining a crowd of friends with a story. Watching his lively expression and his deft hand gestures, Nancy could easily imagine his skill onstage.

"That reminds me," Bess said. "I read through *Tragedie of the Black Knight*. I have to tell you, the riddle wasn't there. In fact, there wasn't a single mention of a black rose in the whole play."

"So Mr. Cole's lead strikes out, Dad," Nancy said.

Bess heaved a big sigh. "It seems like a wild-goose chase, Mr. Drew. We found several black roses, but no secrets behind them."

"No secrets that we could see, anyway," Nancy said. "But there are many different ways a clue could lie 'behind' a rose. Any one of the roses we found could still be hiding our answer."

"The trouble is, we don't know what answer we're looking for," George added. "We don't even know what 'grievous crime' we're hoping to avert."

"I have a feeling it has something to do with the threats Miss Innes is receiving," Nancy said. "I really should turn over to the police the letter I found in her room. But should I confront her with it first, give her a chance to explain things?"

Mr. Drew was about to reply when Pippa hurried up to their table. From the expression on her face, Nancy guessed that she was upset about something.

"Mr. Drew, why did you tell the master about my

anonymous phone call?" Pippa asked. She dropped unhappily into a chair. "Now my father refuses to let me help solve the case anymore."

"I'm sorry," Mr. Drew said. "I was only trying to persuade the master to let you girls search the college. The master dismissed the call as another prank. But your father was with me at the time, and he took the news more seriously. It's not surprising, Pippa. He's concerned for your safety."

"That's why I wasn't going to tell him about the call," Pippa said. "He's such a worrywart. I mean, you're not pulling Nancy off the case just because someone hurled a block of stone at her."

Mr. Drew raised his eyebrows and turned to Nancy. "Someone hurled a block of stone at you?" he asked sharply.

"Oh . . . yes," Nancy replied, feeling sheepish. "I was going to tell you. Bess and I were walking around some back alleys, and a stone block fell off a wall. But neither of us was hurt," she added. "And it just proves, Dad, that this case is serious. I mean, with the thief breaking into Dorothy Innes's apartment and—"

Mr. Drew threw up his hands. "A thief broke in?" he said. "You really have been busy today. Why don't you start from the beginning?"

They took turns recounting the day's events to Mr. Drew. The one thing Nancy didn't mention was Tony's black rose ring. She still wasn't sure how much to tell Pippa of her suspicions about Tony.

They finished just as the waitress returned with big plates of spaghetti and a basket of hot garlic bread. "I can't believe your dad won't let you help us," Bess said to Pippa as she helped herself to the bread. "How can we solve this case without you? You're the one who knows the ins and outs of Boniface College."

Pippa sighed. "And I'd just found another lead, too," she said. "This afternoon, before my father learned about the phone call, he had a look round the Fellows' Garden for us. He tells me there's a black rose growing there—at least, a dark scarlet rose. And the name of the variety is Black Beauty."

Nancy sat up straighter. "That sounds promising," she said.

"But we can't get into the garden," Pippa said, twirling a forkful of spaghetti. "The gate's locked, and my father won't give us his key."

"What danger does he think we'd get into by walking around the Fellows' Garden?" Nancy said. As soon as she said it, though, she thought of one don who might pose some danger: Mr. Sunderwirth.

"He doesn't want me taking chances, as he puts it," Pippa said. "What's more, he knows the master doesn't want us poking about. He doesn't want to antagonize the master."

"And I don't blame your father," Mr. Drew said. "Look, Nancy, maybe you should put this case on the back burner. You don't even know who's asking you to solve the riddle. And you don't know what crime you're trying to prevent."

"Dad, don't tell me you think this is all a prank, too," Nancy said, surprised.

Mr. Drew shook his head. "No, just the opposite. I think it may be *more* serious than you realize. And you don't even know what's at stake. How can you be sure it's worth the risk?"

Nancy clasped her hands together, pleading. "But we don't know that it *isn't* important, either. Please, Dad."

He sighed and shrugged. "I won't forbid you to investigate, Nancy," he said. "I have to rely on your good judgment. Just promise me you won't take any unnecessary chances."

"I promise, Dad," Nancy said.

During the rest of the meal, the group chatted about the sights they'd seen that day—the Ashmolean Museum, the ancient library buildings, the half-timbered pub hidden in a maze of lanes, and the stained-glass windows in St. Cyril's chapel.

After dinner, they left the restaurant and dawdled on the sidewalk. The sun was setting, and darkness was falling over Oxford. "I have to go back to the hotel to make some phone calls to the States," Mr. Drew said. "River Heights is six time zones behind England—it's the middle of the afternoon over there, a good time for me to reach my clients. So what are you all going to do?"

"I thought I'd take them on a walk down to the

river," Pippa said vaguely. But Nancy spotted a gleam in Pippa's eye.

"Fine. I'll see you back at the hotel," Mr. Drew said. He kissed Nancy on the cheek.

As soon as he had left, Nancy turned to Pippa. "That black rose in the garden is too important a clue to pass up," she said decisively.

"I was hoping you'd say that," Pippa said. "No matter what Dad says, I want to stay on this case."

"My dad doesn't want me to go against the master's wishes, either," Nancy said. "But I can't help wondering why Mr. Cole won't let us search the college. If he's involved in a cover-up, the only way to expose him may be to disobey his orders."

"It's not exactly disobeying him," Bess said. "He didn't say we couldn't investigate. He's just not willing to give us keys."

Pippa gave a short, merry laugh. "Well, we will be breaking college rules if we sneak into the Fellows' Garden," she said. "But students do it from time to time, on a dare or as a prank."

"Then what's to stop us?" Nancy said.

The four walked quickly to Boniface. At the gate lodge, they saw Mr. Austin sitting inside. Pippa greeted him cheerfully and stopped to chat. It didn't take her long to get him to lend them a spade. "Thanks. Now we can fix the trampled flower bed under Miss Innes's window," Nancy said with an innocent-looking smile.

With the spade resting on her shoulder, Nancy

strolled with her friends across the moonlit Old Quad. They passed the dining hall, which was dark and shut up for the night, and turned into the main college garden. Avoiding the path, they stayed in the shadows along the edges of the lawn. At the far end, the stage stood ready for tomorrow's play, with rows of empty benches set in front.

"Here's the side wall of the Fellows' Garden," Pippa said, pointing to an ivy-covered stone wall. "Better make sure the coast is clear."

Nancy tiptoed to the corner of the garden wall and peered around. She drew back quickly.

Leaning against the gate of the Fellows' Garden was Mr. Sunderwirth. With his arms folded and one ankle crossed over the other, he looked as if he was set to wait for a while.

Was it just a coincidence? He couldn't possibly be waiting there to catch them—or could he?

Nancy slipped back and reported to her friends. Pippa groaned softly. "There's no danger of him finding us once we're *in* the garden," she said. "Mr. Sunderwirth is only a lecturer—not a full-fledged fellow—so he doesn't have a key to the garden. Still, what if he sees us climbing in?"

"We can't hang around forever," George said. "Someone else may see us standing here with this shovel. I say we go for it."

"I agree," Nancy said.

"All right, but we must be dead quiet," Pippa said.

89

"Want me to stay on this side as a lookout?" Bess asked.

"Good idea," Nancy said. She leaned the spade against the wall and sized up the climb. Then she grasped a stout vine, testing its strength. Bracing one foot against the wall, she began to climb.

It didn't take her long to scale the wall. "Watch out for the top," Nancy called softly as she reached down for the spade. "There's broken glass sticking out, to deter intruders." Picking her way around the sharp glass, Nancy steadied herself and jumped down into the Fellows' Garden.

In a moment, Pippa and George joined her. Using hand signals, they divided the garden among them to search. Pippa chose the area beside the adjacent building, where light streamed from an upper window. Nancy eyed the window uneasily. Clearly someone was right inside there. If that person looked out the window, the girls were sure to be discovered.

But in the section where Nancy was searching, it was too dark to see much. And she didn't dare attract attention by turning on her penlight. All the flowers look black at night, she thought. But we can't come back in the daytime—we'd be spotted climbing over the wall.

The moon sailed out from behind a cloud. Near her feet, Nancy saw a small white marker plunged into the soil. She dropped to her knees to see it closer. Black Beauty, it read.

"George," she whispered, pulling the spade out of her belt. "Over here! This may be it."

George sprinted over. Nancy began digging fast and furiously in the soil behind the rosebush.

Then, suddenly, from the other side of the wall, they heard Bess let out a piercing scream.

10

Digging for Trouble

As Bess's scream split the night, Nancy and George leaped to their feet. Nancy tossed aside the spade and began to run to the wall.

"The gate's quicker!" Pippa called from the other end of the garden. Nancy and George wheeled around and followed Pippa to a tall, moss-covered wooden gate. "You need a key to get in but not to get out," Pippa said breathlessly. She flipped a deadbolt, turned a knob, and flung open the gate.

Out of the corner of her eye, Nancy noticed that Mr. Sunderwirth had disappeared. She also saw a second light snap on in the adjacent building. Somebody threw open a casement window, and a gruff man's voice called, "Who's there?"

But that was the least of her worries at that moment. Nancy and her friends raced around the corner of the garden to where they had left Bess.

She wasn't there.

"Bess!" George called out.

Nancy cast a steady eye over the moonlit garden. Everything looked empty and still. The manicured lawn showed no signs of a struggle.

Pippa echoed George's heartfelt cry. "Bess!"

Listening intently, Nancy thought she heard a muffled grunt, somewhere near the arch leading into the garden from the hall. She dashed off in that direction.

Nancy pounded through the arch into the courtyard by the hall. A flashlight beam came whipping around the passage from the Old Quad. Nancy pressed herself against a wall.

Mr. Austin tramped through the cobblestoned passage, playing a flashlight over the walls. Spotting Nancy, he trained the beam on her. "Hello there," he barked out. Nancy flinched.

Pippa and George galloped through the archway in Nancy's wake. When Mr. Austin saw them, he halted, dropping his flashlight.

"Miss Shaw!" he said. "Tell me that wasn't *you* the master heard messing about in the Fellows' Garden. And to think I trusted you. What were you up to with my garden spade?"

Pippa didn't answer.

Nancy stepped forward. "That's not important now," she said. "Our other friend may have been hurt. Please, can you help us find her?"

Mr. Austin frowned. "Hurt, you say? Where is she?"

The muffled grunt Nancy had heard before rose again. Straining her ears, she guessed it came from the entryway to the dining hall. She sprang over and pushed open the heavy wooden door.

Bess lay in a heap on the stone floor, near the stairs that led up to the minstrel's gallery. When the door opened, her blond head stirred.

"Bess!" Nancy cried, running over to her side.

As Nancy lifted her friend by the shoulders, Bess groaned again. "It's so dark," she mumbled in a woozy voice.

Mr. Austin snapped on the light in the vestibule. "Is she all right?" he asked anxiously.

Bess gave her head a sharp shake. "It's all coming back to me now," she said. "Someone came up from behind and grabbed me. He stuffed a cloth over my nose—it smelled like rubbing alcohol . . ."

"Chloroform, I'll bet," Nancy said. "Just enough to knock you out for a minute or two." She yanked her sweatshirt over her head and wrapped it around Bess, who'd started to shiver. "One side effect is that it lowers your body temperature temporarily. Put this on to stay warm."

"Who could have done this?" Pippa asked.

"A biology student would have easy access to chloroform," Nancy said. "Many labs keep it on hand to anesthetize specimens."

"Wh-whoever it was was f-fairly t-t-tall," Bess said through chattering teeth. "And strong."

Tall, Nancy thought. Like Mr. Sunderwirth? "Did he say anything to you?" she asked Bess.

Bess nodded. "Before I passed out, I heard him growl, 'Tell your friends, curiosity killed the cat,'" she repeated.

Nancy and Pippa traded guilty glances.

"Where did this happen?" Mr. Austin asked.

"Right out in the main garden," Nancy said.

"All the courtyards and quadrangles lead to the garden," Mr. Austin said, scratching his head. "Anyone in the college might have been there. But if it was someone who's not a member of the college, he'll have to pass through the gate to leave Boniface. My wife is tending the gate right now. Anyone who leaves, we'll make him sign the guest book."

"Thanks, Mr. Austin," Pippa said gratefully.

"Shall we report this to the Oxford police?" Mr. Austin asked as Nancy helped Bess to her feet.

Bess shook her head. "He didn't steal anything or hurt me. And I doubt the police could find him without a physical description. Besides"—she winced—"we'd have to admit we were trespassing."

They walked with the porter out of the dining hall. "Well, I'd better swing round and tell the master everything's all right," Mr. Austin said.

Pippa flushed guiltily. "Oh, uh . . ." she stammered. "We left the garden gate wide open."

"And I dropped your spade by the rosebushes," Nancy added. "I'm sorry."

95

"Not to worry. I'll set it all to rights," Mr. Austin said with a wink. "Master needn't know." Swinging his flashlight, he headed for the garden.

"See, I told you he was a love," Pippa said.

"Lucky for us," Nancy said. "Now let's get Bess back to the hotel. We could all use a good night's rest. Who knows what tomorrow will bring?"

Nancy, Bess, and George were at breakfast in the hotel dining room when the waiter called Nancy to the front desk telephone. Pippa was on the line.

"The news is all over college that someone dug a hole in the Fellows' Garden," Pippa said. "Mr. Austin thought he cleared away the evidence, but in the dark, he didn't see the place where you were digging. When the master found it this morning, he was absolutely livid. Apparently he blames it on students—he hasn't connected it to us. But my father suspects something."

"If you need to quit the case, I understand," Nancy said. "Especially if your dad wants you to. But I plan to keep at it."

"Even after what happened to Bess last night?" Pippa asked in surprise.

"Whoever attacked Bess meant to frighten us, not hurt us," Nancy said. "I feel certain he's connected to the black rose, and to the threats you and Miss Innes received. We have to investigate before someone really gets hurt."

"Then count me in," Pippa said. "But we can't

show our faces in college today, not with the master on a rampage. Instead, shall we go punting?"

"Punting?"

"You'll see. Meet me on Boniface Bridge in half an hour."

Nancy hung up and hurried back to fill in Bess and George. They finished breakfast and set out. After a fifteen-minute walk, they joined Pippa on the bridge.

Pippa pointed to the Cherwell River, flowing under the bridge. "Those are punts," she said.

Nancy saw several flat-bottomed boats moored to a small pier by the riverbank. "Are they rowboats?"

"No," Pippa said, leading the Americans to some stairs at the foot of the bridge. "They're more like barges. You push them along with a pole. It's an Oxford tradition, a glorious way to spend a day."

"Sounds perfect," George said.

The boat man on the riverbank soon had them set up. Nancy and Bess sat in the rear of the punt, and George took the middle seat. Standing in the prow, Pippa took a tall pole and pushed off from the dock.

They slid easily up the gentle river, between grassy banks lined with willow trees. After watching Pippa for a while, George begged to try the pole.

"You just push against the river bottom—it's fairly shallow," Pippa said. The punt tipped and wobbled as the two shifted places. "You angle the pole one way or the other to steer."

"I think I've got the hang of it," George said. Her face was set hard in concentration as she thrust the pole down, then lifted it.

Bess sighed deliciously and trailed her hand in the water. "This is so romantic. I wish I were wearing a flowing white dress and a huge straw sun bonnet. And I'd love to have someone like Simon lying beside me, popping grapes into my mouth."

Nancy chuckled at Bess's imagination. Despite her impatience to solve the arrow's riddle, even she was beginning to enjoy the outing.

"If you're lolling on the seat and Simon's feeding you grapes," Pippa said with a giggle, "who's driving the punt?"

George let out a yelp. "My pole's stuck in the mud! I can't pull it out!" The current swung the boat in circles around the pole, as George clung on.

Bess burst out laughing. "I don't care who's driving the punt, so long as it isn't George."

With Pippa's help, George soon freed the pole and got the boat straightened out. Up the river they glided, through dappled sunlight and shade. Before long, they were out of Oxford and into the meadows of the English countryside.

Coming around the bend, Nancy saw an old half-timbered inn set in the middle of a broad, smooth riverside lawn. She peered at the painted wooden sign overhanging the bank. Then she sat up, excited. "You'll never guess what that inn is called," she said. "It's the Black Rose!"

"I can't believe it!" George said. "Quick, Pippa, how do you park this thing?"

"Just steer toward the bank," Pippa said, rising from her seat. "See that wooden landing? I'll jump to shore and haul us in."

In a few minutes, they had tethered the boat to the dock. They climbed out of the punt and walked across the velvety green lawn.

"I remember this pub," Pippa said. "I've ridden up here on the bike path that runs along the river. I never noticed its name before, though."

"The Black Rose has two entrances—one facing the river, the other facing the road," Nancy said, pointing. "Which one's front and which is 'behind'?"

"Whichever way it is," Bess said, studying the grass, "this is another one of those perfect English lawns that hasn't been dug up in decades. Nothing's been buried here recently."

"Maybe there's something behind the sign," Nancy said hopefully. She sprinted over to the waterside signboard and examined it. Then she tried the one by the road. Neither yielded any clues.

Realizing that it was past noon, the four friends sat on the flagstone terrace and ordered some savory meat pies, the inn's specialty. Nancy was surprised to see how much traffic there was on the river—a constant flow of punts on the water and bicycles along the shady riverside path. There was

99

quite a lunchtime crowd at the inn, both inside and out on the terrace. Nancy started for a moment, thinking she had spotted Mr. Sunderwirth at another table. But it turned out to be someone else.

"The punting will be easier going back downstream—the current should push us right along," Pippa said as they returned to their boat after lunch. "Nancy, do you want to try the pole?"

Nancy gamely took the pole and stood in the prow. Following Pippa's advice, she maneuvered them away from the landing and into the stream.

"Don't drift too close to the bank, Nancy," Pippa warned as they swung around the bend. "In some spots, immense tree roots are lurking right below the surface. And the current's awfully strong."

Nancy reached up to push away some trailing willow branches, hanging like a curtain over the river. She leaned far forward to push the pole against a tangle of roots bulging out from the bank.

She heard a sharp, splintering crack. The punt pole had split in two, right in her hands!

Nancy lurched wildly, the boat wobbling beneath her. The punt tipped over—and she plunged into the river.

11

The Play's the Thing

Nancy fought her way to the surface and looked around. Pippa, George, and Bess were treading water, coughing and spluttering from the murky river.

Luckily, the Cherwell was shallow at that point. The girls soon struck bottom with their feet. While Pippa and Bess waded to shore, Nancy and George retrieved the overturned punt and towed it to the riverbank.

Wringing out her sopping wet T-shirt, Bess said, "Now I'm glad I wasn't wearing a flowing white dress. It would have been ruined!"

"The river looks clean when you're on it," Pippa added, "but when you're in it—phew!"

Water streamed down Nancy's red-blond hair, plastering it to her neck and shoulders. Her muddy sneakers went *squish-squosh* as she paced along the bank, staring into the tangled tree roots.

"Nancy, next to you I look like an ace punter," George said. "Maybe I sent us spinning in circles, but at least I didn't dump us in the river."

"Sorry I gave you all a dunking," Nancy said, "but look here."

Leaning over, she pulled the stump of the pole out of the tree roots. She held up the broken end.

"Look at the base of the split," she said, pointing to the pale exposed wood. "The cut is smooth and clean. And look at these serrated marks—as if someone had used a tiny saw. Someone cut the pole halfway through, knowing it would split apart under the stress of punting."

George looped the mooring rope around a tree, then stepped over to inspect the pole. She frowned. "When I was holding the pole, I didn't notice anything."

"Neither did I," Pippa said. "And it didn't break when George got it stuck in the mud."

Nancy nodded. "Someone must have tampered with it while we were at the Black Rose. There were so many people around, it would have been easy."

"Someone might have watched us get in the punt back in Oxford," George said, "then followed us on the bike path. There's a thick row of trees between the path and the river. We wouldn't have seen him."

"But who would have done that?" Pippa asked,

eyes filling with tears. "I'm frightened, Nancy. First the phone call, then the falling stone, then the attack in the garden last night. And now this."

Nancy sat down on the grassy riverbank. "I have to assume that this person who's threatening us also wants to know where the black rose is. So why scare us off when we haven't found it yet?"

"You think the person who sent the riddle is the same person who's threatening us?" Bess said.

"I doubt it," Nancy said. "Why get us started, then scare us off before we find it? No, I think we're being threatened by another person—one who knows about the black rose, but doesn't know where it is, either."

"Maybe," said George. "But in that case, why not let us do the finding, and *then* stop us? Someone deliberately set us on this trail, and I think we were picked because we're experienced investigators. So why not let us find the rose for them?"

Nancy thought for a second. "Maybe we've already found it, and we just didn't recognize it."

"But how are we going to recognize it?" Bess asked. "We looked behind every black rose we've seen. Maybe there was some proof of a grievous crime we could avert. But it hasn't exactly jumped out and bitten us on the nose."

"I know, I know," Nancy said. "I've never had a case before that made me feel so stupid."

"Speaking of feeling stupid," Pippa said, "we'll look pretty stupid if we just sit here in wet clothes all afternoon. It'll be hard punting without a pole, but the current should carry us back down to the bridge. That'll be faster than walking back."

"We need to return the boat anyway," Nancy said. "I'm game. How about you guys?"

"Let's go," George said. She untied the punt.

Bess sighed. "Well, I'm not walking back by myself," she said. "But I get first dibs on the shower when we get back to the hotel room. I can't go to the play tonight stinking of river muck!'

As Pippa had promised, the Boniface garden made a romantic outdoor theater. At seven o'clock, it was still well before sunset. Velvety shadows had begun to gather, but the reddish gold evening sunlight still slanted brightly across the lawn.

Bess had put on a billowy white blouse and a long wine-colored skirt that draped around her hips. A black velvet headband skimmed back her blond hair. "I always think this outfit makes me look like Juliet in *Romeo and Juliet*," she said. "Do you think Simon will be able to see me from the stage?"

Pippa giggled. "Not a chance," she said. "He won't be able to see past the footlights. Besides, Bess, you have a lot of competition tonight. I'll bet half the audience is his female fans."

Looking around, Nancy grinned. All the front benches were filled with young women, dressed up and craning their necks eagerly toward the stage.

"Say, there's Tony," George said, "in one of the back rows." Nancy twisted around and spotted Tony behind them. He waved and grinned. Nancy waved back with a twinge of anxiety. Why did Tony pop up wherever they went?

Pippa pivoted around to wave, too. "I wonder if Tony has any news about Miss Innes's break-in."

Nancy traded cautious looks with George. She had confided her suspicions about Tony to George and Bess, and she'd told them about his signet ring with the black rose. But she'd decided not to tell Pippa, knowing how loyal Pippa was to Tony.

Spooky recorded music signaled that the play was beginning. "We can talk to him after the play," Pippa whispered, turning to face the stage again.

A crowd of young men in doublets and tights rushed onto the stage, and the play was off and running. Despite the old-fashioned language, Nancy found it easy to follow the plot. It was a rip-roaring melodrama, full of murders, sword fights, and intrigue. For the next two hours, Nancy forgot all about black roses.

And watching Simon in action, she couldn't help but be impressed. His slim figure moved confidently onstage, and he had a commanding stage voice. With a toss of his brown hair or a flash from his gray eyes, he convinced her of his passion in the love scenes and his courage in the action scenes.

At last, clutching a dagger that had been plunged into his chest, Simon gasped out his death speech. "And so I go to my grave," he proclaimed, "but sorrow not for me. For there I meet my lady love, for all eternity." Then, with a groan, he sank to the floor and closed his eyes.

The garden broke out in mad applause. Nancy joined in. Bess was wiping tears from her cheeks. Onstage, Simon popped up, still with the fake dagger in his chest, to take his bows.

"I'd like to go backstage and say hello to my friend Claire," Pippa said, rising to her feet. "She played the sister of the evil duke. She was at school with Tony and me. Want to come?"

"You bet," Bess said eagerly.

"Why not?" Nancy agreed.

Behind the makeshift stage, the actors stood around greeting their friends. Pippa spotted her friend Claire untying the laced-up bodice of her dress. "I can't wait to get out of this hot velvet gown," she told Pippa as they hugged. "Why did we do a full-dress costume drama in the middle of summer?"

"You know why," grumbled the student who'd played the evil duke. He was peeling off a fake beard. "His Lordship, Master Simon, wanted to show off his legs in tights."

Claire punched his shoulder playfully. "Come on, David, you have to admit that Simon was brilliant."

"I'll grant you that," he replied. "But he would have been just as brilliant in *Julius Caesar*. And then *we* could have worn nice airy Roman togas."

Nancy and her friends laughed as the "duke" went over to meet some of his friends.

Pippa introduced her American friends to Claire. As they chatted, Tony joined them.

"You did a great job, Claire," he said, kissing her cheek.

"Thanks, Tony," she said. "I'm just glad it didn't rain. Performing outdoors, you always take that risk. But it turned out to be gorgeous tonight."

"Tony, any word about Miss Innes?" Pippa asked.

"Nothing much," he said. "I went past her rooms this morning to check that she's all right. She said the police hadn't found any clues about the break-in, except for the broken window. But nothing else was stolen. It seems obvious the thief was after the manuscript, but for some reason he didn't take it."

Nancy noticed that Bess wasn't paying attention to Tony. Her ears were straining in the direction of Simon Coningsby, who stood nearby surrounded by a circle of female admirers.

"Of course, it isn't a very good play—as literature, at least," Simon was saying in an authoritative voice. "If you didn't have good actors, it would be an utter bore. But I cut out a few scenes to make the action flow better, and I rewrote some lines here and there."

"So he's a talented writer, too," Bess murmured, starry-eyed.

"Oh, Simon will be rich and famous someday, no doubt about it," Claire said in an undertone. "As if he needed the money. He just inherited a fortune, you know."

Bess's eyes bugged out. "Really?"

Claire nodded. "He's the grandson of that famous mystery writer who died recently," she said.

Nancy perked up. "Dame Gwyneth Davies?"

"That's the one," Claire said. "Someone told me that he was her sole heir. His mother was Davies's only child, his parents have both died, and he has no brothers or sisters."

"Wow," Nancy said. "So he probably inherited the royalties from her books, too. After all these years, they're still best-sellers, you know. Every time a Gwyneth Davies novel is sold, that'll be money in Simon's pocket."

"Not to mention the profit from *The Monkey Puzzle*," Pippa added. "If that play continues to be a hit, he could become quite rich indeed."

"Some blokes have all the luck," Tony muttered.

Nancy stole a glance at him and saw his dark eyes smoldering with envy. What was it with him and Simon? she wondered.

"That reminds me, Nancy, did you ever pick up tickets for *The Monkey Puzzle?*" Pippa asked.

Nancy shook her head. "With all the excitement yesterday afternoon, I forgot."

But her mind wasn't on the conversation anymore. The news about Simon had set off a warning signal. Both Simon and Miss Innes had close connections to the late Dame Gwyneth. Why did that seem like more than a coincidence to her?

Nancy noticed Bess pushing through the crowd surrounding Simon, holding out her program from the play. "Simon, would you mind signing this?" she asked, with a mushy grin on her face. Sparked by curiosity about Simon, Nancy crowded up behind Bess.

Simon turned and gave Bess a conceited smile. With a flourish, he reached out his left hand to take the program. "Shall I inscribe it to you, Bess?" he asked.

Nancy froze and gasped.

On Simon's finger glinted a black onyx ring—the exact twin of Tony's. Did this one have a black rose on it, too?

12

A Ring of Suspects

Nancy darted over to where Bess was standing. "Yes, please," Bess was saying sweetly.

"To Bess, with all best wishes," Simon recited as he scrawled on her program. He handed it back to her. "And you, Nancy?" he asked, eyebrows raised.

"No autograph for me, thanks," Nancy said. Then, realizing that sounded rude, she added, "But I thought you were terrific in the play."

"Thanks," Simon said. He smiled, but his keen gray eyes seemed to study her for a second.

Nancy's mind raced. What excuse could she find to inspect Simon's ring? She felt she had to check it out, and Simon was about to turn away.

"Is that ring part of your costume, or is it your own?" she asked.

"Ring?" Simon asked. He appeared confused for a moment. Then he looked down at his hands. On the right hand, he was wearing a ruby so big it had to be a stage prop.

"The signet ring," Nancy said. "I'm just asking because a friend of mine has one like it."

"No, it's my own," Simon replied, looking up at her coldly. "But I thought it suited the character."

"I get it—Black Knight, black ring," Nancy said. She grabbed Simon's hand. "And what's that design on the signet? A family crest?" It was a rose, exactly like Tony's.

Simon pulled his hand back. "No, it's a flower of some kind," he said in an offhand tone.

"Nancy, come on," Bess whispered.

Nancy knew she was embarrassing her friend. But she just couldn't think of a way to get Simon to let her check his ring for a secret compartment.

"It does fit the part," she said, stalling for time. "Imagine the Black Knight hiding poison in a secret compartment in a ring like that."

"Good idea for a sequel," Simon said dryly. "We'll bring him miraculously back to life and call it *Tragedie of the Black Knight 2—The Revenge.*"

Bess giggled nervously. "Just like they do in Hollywood."

Simon smiled faintly. "Thank you so much for coming tonight. Now, if you'll excuse me . . ." He turned his back on Nancy and Bess and began talking to some other fans.

"Nancy, how could you do that!" Bess said as they returned to their friends. "Now he'll think I'm a geek."

"I'm sorry, Bess," Nancy said. "But his ring looks just like Tony's—it's got a black rose on it. I had to try to find out whether something could be hidden behind that rose."

Nancy turned and looked through the crowd at Simon. Laughing, he was holding a red-haired girl's hand and squeezing it fondly.

But as he released it, Nancy saw him glance down at his own hand. Although he kept chatting, he casually slipped the signet ring from his finger. He tilted it and stuck a finger inside, as if checking for a secret compartment. Finding nothing, he slid the ring on again.

That tells me two things, Nancy thought. One, there's nothing behind the rose on Simon's ring.

And two, Simon knows what we're looking for.

At the hotel that night, Mr. Drew passed on an invitation for Nancy and her friends. Mrs. Cole— the master's wife—had asked them to go on a cross-country horseback ride in the Cotswolds. "Sounds like fun!" George said.

"Great," Mr. Drew said. "She said she'll pick you up here, in her car, at nine tomorrow morning."

Nancy frowned. "I'll bet the master asked her to get us out of his hair."

"Nan, that's not fair," Mr. Drew said. "She asked me herself, at tea in the Senior Common Room this afternoon."

Nancy sat up with an idea. "George, you and

Bess should go riding," she said. "And while you're there, pump Mrs. Cole for information. Get the lowdown on Miss Innes and on Mr. Sunderwirth. I still don't trust that guy."

"You bet," George said. "And maybe we can even get Mrs. Cole to persuade her husband to let us investigate."

"Aren't you coming, Nancy?" Bess asked. "A horseback ride has to be better than aimlessly searching for black roses."

"No, thanks," Nancy said. "I agree, we haven't gotten very far in our hunt. But the Gwyneth Davies connection is starting to intrigue me. I have a hunch that I want to pursue."

So the next morning, as soon as George and Bess rode off in Mrs. Cole's car, Nancy set off on foot for the Oxford library. Eventually, she found the reading room where current books were kept. As she'd expected, there was an entire shelf of Dame Gwyneth's mysteries.

Nancy had already read most of Davies's work, so it was easy to skim through the novels. She hoped something would jog her thinking and give her some kind of a lead.

An hour passed, then two. Nancy became increasingly excited. In book after book, she found references to black roses—embroidery on a handkerchief, petals pressed in a dead woman's locket, the name of a song that a murderer was heard whistling. None of the images stood out strongly on its own, but taken together they *had* to mean something, Nancy told herself.

Leaning back in her chair, Nancy paused to think. She held a copy of Dame Gwyneth's sixth book, *Death Takes the Morning Train.* Musing, she turned the book over and slipped off the dust jacket.

There was a rose embossed on the black binding!

Nancy jumped up and went back to the bookshelf. She checked the cover of book after book. The first two volumes had plain covers, but after that all of them carried the rose.

Dame Gwyneth must have considered the black rose her personal symbol, Nancy reflected, leaning against the bookcase. After a couple of best-sellers, the publishers could have agreed to stamp it on her books. That kind of thing would have appealed to a member of the Puzzlers.

And if the black rose was her symbol, Nancy realized, she probably had also had it engraved on a signet ring for her grandson, Simon Coningsby.

But then how did Tony get a matching ring?

Shaking her head, Nancy slipped the last book back on the shelf. If Dame Gwyneth were still alive, she told herself, I'd think that the message on the arrow had come from her. But she's been dead for two months. A corpse can't shoot an arrow.

Then her heart skipped a beat. What if the corpse's best friend shot the arrow—bearing a message from beyond the grave?

An image popped into Nancy's mind—the

paperweight she'd seen on Miss Innes's desk. It was a goddess with a bow and arrow. Nancy tried to remember the mythology she had studied in school. The Roman goddess of the hunt was named Diana. Suppose Dorothy Innes had taken Diana as her Puzzler symbol, because she herself was a skilled archer. Even though Miss Innes was in a wheelchair, her upper body might still be strong. People kept saying she was frail, but Nancy had seen her wheel that chair around vigorously.

Nancy snapped her fingers. "If I can get a sample of her handwriting," she said softly, "I can compare it to the message that was attached to the arrow. And I know just who might have a sample!"

Nancy hurried out of the library and jogged over to Boniface. At the gate lodge, she stopped to ask Mr. Austin where Tony's room was.

"Right across the Old Quad," Mr. Austin said. "Staircase Ten, Room Four."

Thanking him, Nancy sprinted off across the quad in the direction he'd indicated. She soon located the sign for Staircase Ten and turned into the open doorway. A well-worn stone staircase wound upward into dim, cool shadows.

The door nearest to the stairway entrance cracked open. Nancy heard Mr. Sunderwirth's voice say, "When you come next week, bring me an essay on Victor Hugo . . ."

Nancy ducked back out of the doorway. To her right, a pair of arched windows looked out onto the quad. Inside, she could see a book-lined study. Mr.

Sunderwirth was sitting at the desk. When he turned his head, he spotted her. Looking startled, he leaped to his feet.

Nancy dashed away, heading for the lodge. If Mr. Sunderwirth was responsible for the recent threats and attack, she didn't want him to catch her snooping around. "Mr. Austin," she called as she reached the lodge's window, "can I use the phone to call Tony instead?"

Mr. Austin looked surprised, but he handed her the phone. "Dial four-six-three-three," he said.

On the first ring, Tony answered. "D'Souza here."

"Hi, Tony, it's Nancy Drew," she said, still out of breath. "Don't think I'm crazy, but—do you have an old history paper I could look at?"

"Well, sure, but . . ." Tony sounded baffled.

"I'm at the gate," Nancy said. "And, uh, I'd rather not come up to your room. Please don't ask why. Can you come down and meet me?"

Tony paused a moment, and Nancy was afraid he would question her. But instead he said, "Why don't we meet on Boniface Bridge in ten minutes?"

Why wait ten minutes? Nancy wondered. And why arrange the meeting for farther away, when she was only a few steps from his room?

"Well, if you really want to—" she said.

"That way, I can show you the view from Boniface Tower," Tony said in a cheerful voice. "It's got a great bird's-eye view of Oxford. I was thinking last night that you should see it before you leave."

"Okay, fine, ten minutes," Nancy said. " 'Bye!"

After thanking Mr. Austin again, Nancy jogged across the quad in the other direction. Ten minutes should give her enough time to trace the route from Miss Innes's rooms to the minstrel's gallery. She headed toward Miss Innes's office, then turned off on the side corridor to the elevator. The elevator was locked, so Nancy ran up the stairs and down the corridor next to the library.

Opening the second-story door, Nancy stepped out onto the minstrel's gallery. A buzz of talk and lunchtime aromas rose from the dining hall below. She looked down on the students and dons eating their meal.

"Miss Innes could have left the Common Room, gone to her office to fetch a bow and arrow, and come back up here," Nancy said to herself. "She parked her chair by the railing, shot the arrow, then wheeled immediately out of sight." She remembered the billow of dark cloth she'd seen in the gallery Tuesday night when the arrow came whistling down.

Checking her watch, Nancy realized she had to hurry to meet Tony. No time to go around the back way. She slipped down the stairs leading to the dining hall lobby. A few students were strolling in and out, but no one seemed to notice Nancy emerge from the stairway. She trotted across the lobby and out into the courtyard.

Nancy ran most of the way to Boniface Bridge. When she reached the meeting spot, she came to a stop and looked around. Tony was nowhere to be seen. She knew she was a couple of minutes late, but surely Tony would have waited for her.

Leaning over the stone railing, Nancy tried to catch her breath. Below her, she saw the fleet of punts moored to their dock. A crow swooped up from the dock with a harsh caw.

Nancy idly followed the crow's line of flight. As it soared upward, Nancy noticed Boniface Tower for the first time. It was a slender turret of golden stone, rising beside the foot of the bridge.

She broke into a smile of relief. There was Tony, leaning over a small balcony high up on the tower, waving to her.

She straightened up and waved back, making sign language to Tony—should she try to find her way up, or would he come down? Tony gestured toward the door in the base of the tower. Then his fingers imitated her walking up the stairs.

But a second later she saw Tony pitch forward and tumble over the railing—plummeting straight toward the river.

13

Falling into Danger

Stifling a scream, Nancy ran forward. Although the tower stood right at the river's edge, the punt dock jutted out into the water beneath Tony. If he fell on it, he could break his neck!

By some miracle Tony managed to grab a stone gargoyle on a ledge halfway up the tower. Of course, Nancy remembered. Tony was a gymnast.

Tony's fingers clenched hard as he tried to pull himself up. For a frightening moment, his hands slipped again. But then Tony threw an arm over the gargoyle's neck and braced himself.

"Tony!" Nancy shouted to him. "Hang on—I'll get help!"

"Hurry!" Tony called back. He grunted with effort as he desperately tried to hold on.

Nancy sprinted back to the college gate to fetch Mr. Austin. Without delay, the porter grabbed a

119

rope and ran with her to the base of the tower. The small wooden door stood open. They raced up the narrow iron stairs winding to the top.

Having burst into the small, round observation room, Nancy dashed over to the open window and stepped out onto the small balcony. Mr. Austin joined her. Leaning over the stone railing, she saw Tony clinging to the gargoyle, about fifteen feet below. A curious crowd had already gathered on the sidewalk, staring up at the dangling figure.

After swiftly tying the rope in a loop, Mr. Austin began feeding it over the railing. "Put this around your waist," he called down to Tony. "You get hold of the other end," he ordered Nancy.

When the rope reached Tony, he wriggled around, trying to stick his head and arms through the loop without letting go. Nancy could read the strain on his face.

At last Tony managed to get the rope around himself. Mr. Austin tightened it with a smart tug. Then he and Nancy began to haul the rope up, hand over hand.

Tony's body bounced and scraped against the tower wall as they pulled him up. Finally, Mr. Austin reached over the railing and grabbed Tony by the shoulders. Nancy held the rope taut until Tony tumbled safely over the railing. A spatter of applause erupted from the onlookers below.

Drawing deep breaths, Tony lay still on the stone

for a minute. Nancy knelt beside him. Mr. Austin rubbed his back.

"You—you saved my life," Tony finally was able to say.

"You saved your own life," Nancy said. "Lucky for you that gargoyle was there."

"I couldn't have held on much longer," Tony declared. He rolled over onto his back.

"What happened, Mr. D'Souza?" Mr. Austin asked.

Tony screwed shut his eyes. "I was pushed. I was leaning out over the railing, and somebody came up from behind and pushed me."

"Do you know who it was?" Nancy asked.

Tony shook his head. "Someone must have followed me up the stairs," he replied. "I didn't hear anybody, but I was leaning outside—the traffic noise would have covered the sound of footsteps."

"I didn't see anyone come out of the tower," Nancy said. "But someone could have crept downstairs and slipped out while I was running to get Mr. Austin."

"The tower is always open," Mr. Austin said. "Anyone could get in, I suppose."

"But why would anyone push me?" Tony wondered, slowly sitting up. "I could have been killed."

Nancy sat back on her heels, trying to quell her lingering suspicion of Tony. He had been the one to propose this odd meeting place. Could he have staged the incident himself? As a gymnast, he might have known he could catch himself after the fall. Had he made himself look like a target in order to throw her off his trail?

Then her eyes fell again on Tony's signet ring. The ring had to be a clue of some kind. What was Tony's connection to the black rose?

And would Simon—the owner of the other black rose ring—soon be a victim, too?

When he was certain Tony was safe, Mr. Austin took the rope and went back to the gate lodge. Before she and Tony left, Nancy inspected the tower room and the stairs for clues, but she found nothing.

"Oh, no!" Tony exclaimed, coming to a stop on the sidewalk outside the tower.

"Tony, what is it?" Nancy asked, worried.

"When I fell, I dropped the history paper I brought for you to see," Tony said. He began to search around anxiously. "It must have fallen somewhere near here. Help me look."

As she searched the area with Tony, Nancy wondered again if he had staged his fall. If he didn't want her to check Miss Innes's handwriting on his paper, it would have been a convenient way to prevent her. Then she shook her head, annoyed with herself. Tony could have simply refused to show her the paper. That would have been easier than jumping out of a tower. My suspicions are running away with me, Nancy thought.

Eventually, she spied a white mass floating at the

river's edge. They went down the steps to the punt dock to pull it out. Tony lifted up a soggy heap of paper. His typewritten essay was still readable, but only a faint blur remained of Miss Innes's handwritten notes.

Nancy tried to hide her disappointment. "I'm sorry, Tony," she said. "It wasn't all that important. I only wanted a sample of Miss Innes's handwriting."

As she said this, she wondered if Tony would ask her why. But he didn't seem curious. "Miss Innes's handwriting?" he said. "Oh, I've got plenty of samples of that. She scribbles endless comments on my papers. Come back to my room, and I'll show you some."

Thinking for a second, Nancy decided it was worth the risk of running into Mr. Sunderwirth. Following up the clue of the handwriting was too important to delay any more. And if Tony was so eager to help her out, maybe she could rule him off her suspect list after all. "Okay. Thanks, Tony," she said.

Tony and Nancy walked in silence through the gate and across the Old Quad. He led her up the worn stone stairs of Staircase Ten. On each floor was a small, dark landing with two doors. When they reached the fourth floor, Tony pushed open one of the doors.

They stepped into a large, messy sitting room with rough plaster walls and heavy oak furniture. A group of shabby armchairs faced a fireplace. Books and papers were piled high on a massive wooden desk. Crossing over to a set of small-paned windows, Nancy looked out at a splendid view of the river.

Tony bent over to plug in an electric kettle, which was on the floor. "I'll make us tea and sandwiches," he said. "I don't feel like eating in hall today."

He went into a side room, and Nancy peered through the doorway. She saw a tiny bedroom, just big enough for a single bed and a dresser. Not a bad setup for a student, she thought.

Tony came back, juggling a loaf of bread, a hunk of cheese, some apples, and another typewritten paper. He dropped the food on a small oak table and tossed the paper to Nancy. "Check it out," he said.

Nancy unfolded the paper and scanned the handwriting on it. "Shallow analysis," his teacher had written. "With your training and intelligence, I expect you to dig deeper."

Tony gave a rueful grin. "She's pretty hard to please," he said. "I wanted to show you one that makes me look clever, but there aren't any."

Nancy smiled at Tony. But as she bent over the paper, she wasn't thinking of Miss Innes's opinion of Tony's work. She studied the tiny, precise script, checking out its loops, slants, and curves.

It certainly looks like the handwriting on the arrow's message, Nancy thought with rising excitement. But she'd have to compare them side by side to be sure.

Tony had taken out a bread knife and was hacking off slices from the loaf. "Why is this so important to you, Nancy?" he asked casually. "Does it have anything to do with the black roses you and Pippa were hunting for?"

Keeping her eyes down, Nancy tried to think of a plausible excuse. Before she could answer, though, footsteps pounded up the stairway. She and Tony both turned as fists hammered on the thick oak door.

Tony trotted over and opened the door. There stood Pippa, looking wild-eyed.

"Nancy—at last I found you," she said, out of breath and panting. "Your father rang our house looking for you. I ran over on the chance you might be in Boniface. Mr. Austin said he thought you'd be here."

Nancy jumped to her feet. "Pippa, what is it?"

"Mrs. Cole just phoned from the Cotswolds," Pippa said. "She's bringing George back right away—and going straight to the hospital."

"Hospital?" Nancy and Tony echoed together.

Pippa nodded. "George was thrown off the horse she was riding. A black mare—and guess what its name was?"

Nancy shivered. Somehow she knew the answer. "Rose!"

14

A Rose Is a Rose

"Another black rose!" Tony exclaimed. "Really, Nancy, you've got to tell me what's going on now. I fall out of a tower, George gets thrown from a horse—this can't be coincidence."

"You fell out of a tower?" Pippa asked Tony.

"I'll explain on the way to the hospital," Nancy said with a sigh.

Tony and Nancy grabbed their cheese sandwiches and headed out the door with Pippa. As they walked across Oxford, Nancy told Pippa about Tony's accident. Then she went back to the beginning and told Tony the facts of the case so far—the riddle attached to the arrow, and the danger the girls had met while searching for a black rose.

The hospital was a rambling gray stone building on a busy street in north Oxford. After crossing a cobbled courtyard, Nancy, Pippa, and Tony went in through the emergency entrance. Bess, Mr. Drew, and Mrs. Cole were waiting there on a padded bench.

"Nancy!" Bess called out, jumping to her feet. "Did Pippa tell you?"

"Is George all right?" Nancy asked anxiously.

"The doctor's examining her now," Mrs. Cole said. "The fall knocked her out, but she came to quickly, thank goodness. Still, I wanted a doctor to look at her. I don't want to take any chances."

"The horse's name was Rose, Nancy," Bess said. "And she was black. Black Rose. That's why George chose her, of all the horses in the stable."

"I thought the mare was too high-strung and skittish," Mrs. Cole said, "but George said she could manage her. And she did pretty well at first. We went out on a hillside bridle trail, and everything was fine—until that car came along."

Nancy flinched. "What car?"

Bess shot her a meaningful look. "A snappy little black sports car came hurtling down the road. I swear it was heading straight for us."

"The horse bolted," Mrs. Cole said, "and George was knocked off by a low-hanging tree limb. The fall in itself wasn't so bad, but that branch gave her head a nasty crack."

A swinging door opened, and George walked out, dressed in jeans and a sweatshirt. A gray-haired doctor followed her. "Miss Fayne looks just fine," the doctor said. "She'll have a big bruise on her forehead, that's all."

"Thank you so much, Doctor," Mr. Drew said, shaking her hand.

"Nancy, did you hear?" George said as the doctor left. "I was riding a black rose—"

"The name of your horse may have been a coincidence, George," Nancy said grimly, "but the accident wasn't. Someone was trying to get you."

Mrs. Cole's jaw dropped. "Why would someone try to hurt George?" she asked.

Nancy turned to Mrs. Cole. "Do you remember Tuesday night, in the dining hall, when that arrow came flying down?" she asked.

Mrs. Cole nodded. Nancy proceeded to give her a brief rundown of the case so far. "We'd like to search the college for clues," she finished, "but the master won't let us. And meanwhile, 'accidents' like this keep happening to me and my friends."

Mrs. Cole pressed her lips firmly together. "He won't let you investigate, will he? Well, we'll see about that." Then she swept out the doorway. Pausing only to say goodbye to Nancy's father, Nancy, Bess, George, Pippa, and Tony trotted after her.

The five young people piled into Mrs. Cole's minivan and drove to Boniface, wheeling in through a back gate. They marched over to the master's lodgings, which overlooked the Fellows' Garden.

Mr. Cole looked up, surprised, when his wife barged into his wood-paneled office. "Edgar, what's the meaning of this?" she demanded. "Miss Drew and her friends want to search for clues to answer this riddle. While you're blocking their investigation, somebody is trying to stop them. They've been nearly clobbered with a block of stone, drowned in the Cherwell, suffocated in the garden, and splatted on the pavement by Boniface Tower."

Nancy stifled a grin. Mrs. Cole certainly had a dramatic way of putting things.

"If things are getting dangerous," Mr. Cole said stiffly, "the girls should give up their search. Or perhaps you ought to inform the Oxford police, Miss Drew," he added, turning to her. "I could get Inspector Morris on the phone right now."

Nancy shook her head stubbornly. "We're not trying to find the rose to save our own skins," she said. "The riddle hinted that someone has been hurt by a crime, and I think I know who it is. I believe that Miss Innes is being harassed for some reason, and the arrow was part of the scheme."

Mr. Cole cleared his throat. "I know all about it," he said calmly.

"You do?" Nancy was taken aback.

He nodded. "Miss Innes came to me three weeks ago. She says someone's been writing her threatening letters and making unnerving telephone calls to her."

"And you didn't do anything about it, Edgar?" Mrs. Cole asked, looking shocked.

129

"She refused to let me contact the police," Mr. Cole said with a shrug. "She's a stubborn woman, as you may have noticed. So I did the only thing I could think of. I assigned another member of the faculty to keep an eye on her. It's Mark Sunderwirth, our lecturer in French literature. He manages to sit near her at meals, check her college mailbox, drop by her room occasionally to see how she's doing. His rooms are just across the quad from hers, so he can keep watch out his windows."

Nancy drew a deep breath. So that was why Mr. Sunderwirth had been prowling around the minstrel's gallery, carrying the note to Miss Innes, and lurking in the gardens. It all made sense now.

Mr. Cole gave her a steely gaze. "So you see, I have things under control," he said. "I don't need to give you the keys to the college, or let you rip up the paneling in the hall. Now, if that's all . . ."

Glumly, Nancy, Bess, George, Pippa, and Tony thanked Mr. and Mrs. Cole and trooped out of the office. "What's next?" Tony asked as they plopped down on the grass in the main garden.

"Time to question Dorothy Innes," Nancy said. "Mr. Cole may think he's got things under control, but I bet Miss Innes doesn't. Otherwise, why would she shoot that arrow to pull us into the case?"

"Miss Innes shot the arrow?" Bess looked incredulous.

Nancy filled them in on her discoveries in the library.

"A riddle attached to an arrow—that's just Miss

Innes's style," Tony said. "She was one of the Puzzlers, after all."

"You can't really think that old woman could have shot the arrow, Nancy," Pippa said.

"I believe it," Tony declared. "She can't walk, but she's wiry and strong otherwise." He snapped his fingers. "Now that I think of it, she does have a bow and arrow hanging over her fireplace. I've stared at it often enough during my tutorials."

Nancy was surprised. "I didn't see any bow and arrow when I was there."

"Maybe she hid the bow after she shot the arrow at you," Tony said.

Nancy jumped to her feet. "If the master won't let us search her rooms, maybe *she* will. Come on!"

"Do you really think she'll let us in, Nan?" George asked as they followed Nancy. "That first night in the Senior Common Room, as soon as Miss Innes learned you were a detective, she clammed up and left the room."

"I'll bet she was in a hurry to go find some way to send me an anonymous message," Nancy said. "If she's being harassed, she would've been afraid to talk to me directly."

"But when we came to her with the manuscript, she rushed us out awfully rudely," Tony said.

"If she's being watched," George said, "she wouldn't want us to be connected with her."

"Right after we left her rooms, I got that anonymous phone call," Pippa said. "So maybe someone *was* watching." She shivered.

131

They jogged past the hall and across the Old Quad to Miss Innes's apartment. But when they knocked, there was no answer.

Disappointed, Nancy checked her watch. "It's nearly four o'clock," she said. "Dad's lecture to the Common Law Society is tonight. We can't miss that. And George and Bess and I promised we'd have dinner with him beforehand."

"Well, Miss Innes isn't going anywhere," Tony said. "We can meet back here in the morning. And maybe then this whole mystery will be solved."

Mr. Drew had chosen an Indian restaurant for dinner. Sitar music played over the sound system, and a mural of the Taj Mahal hung on the wall near their table. Soon after they ordered, a waiter brought a steaming bowl of rice to their table, along with hot flatbreads and several spicy curries.

Nancy brought Mr. Drew up to date on the latest developments in the case. He listened thoughtfully. "You said it's possible that you've already found the black rose but didn't know it," he said. "Maybe it would help to review all the roses you've found."

"Okay," Nancy said. "First, there was the crest on the dining hall wall. Then there were the roses in the Wycherly manuscript—but since the thief tossed it aside, it's probably not what we're looking for. Then there was Miss Innes's rose brooch, a gift from Gwyneth Davies, by the way."

"But Miss Innes wouldn't have needed us to search for that," George said.

"Then there was the rose window in the college chapel," Bess said. "Only it wasn't in Boniface—it was in St. Cyril's College."

"Does the rose have to be in Boniface?" Mr. Drew asked, helping himself to more chicken curry.

Nancy considered this. "I guess not."

George leaned forward. "Nan, didn't Miss Innes say Gwyneth Davies taught at St. Cyril's?" she said.

"Why, yes," Nancy said. "So it might have a strong connection for Miss Innes. But there was nothing behind that window—just sky."

"Except . . ." Bess said, frowning intently. "When light shines through a stained-glass window, doesn't it cast an image on the ground?"

Nancy smacked herself on the forehead. "Of course!" she said. "And something could be hidden in the floor behind that image."

"Let's go look!" Bess said excitedly.

"Whoa, there," Mr. Drew said. "It's almost dark. And you do have a lecture to go to."

"Of course, Dad," Nancy said. "We'll go after your lecture—when the moon comes up."

But Nancy barely touched the rest of her dinner. As they walked to the lecture hall, she and her friends could talk of nothing else but the rose. They dutifully sat down and tried to concentrate on Mr. Drew's talk. But if he hadn't been such a good speaker, they wouldn't have absorbed a word.

As soon as the lecture was over, the three friends scurried to the door of the lecture hall. After

133

waving to Mr. Drew over the heads of the crowd, they dashed out and headed for St. Cyril's.

The main gates were shut, but a smaller door to the side was open. The porter, recognizing Nancy and Bess, waved them on. Moonlight flooded the front quad. They jogged to the chapel, easing open its heavy door.

As soon as they entered the chapel, they saw the rose window glowing richly in the moonlight.

Just as they'd hoped, the shape of the rose fell squarely on a paving stone in the chapel floor.

15

The Rose's Secret

"Nancy, it worked!" Bess said eagerly. "Whatever is under that stone is 'behind' the rose."

Nancy knelt down to examine the stone. "And look here," she said. "The mortar around this stone is fresh and new, while all the surrounding stones have crumbled mortar. I'd say somebody put this stone in place not so very long ago."

"Who would have done that?" George asked.

Nancy shrugged. "The porter said St. Cyril's chapel was renovated," she said. "The builders were probably repairing a broken stone."

Nancy fished a pocketknife out of her purse. Flipping out the largest blade, she worked it around the edge of the stone. "This stone is at least three inches thick," she said. "We need a crowbar to raise it." She sat back on her heels.

"Somehow I don't think the porter will lend us

one," Bess said. "He's friendly enough, but he's bound to ask what we're doing. And he'd hit the roof if we told him the truth."

"Renovation is still going on in the rear quad," Nancy recalled. "Maybe there are some tools by the building site."

The three hurried back to the door. It took a little shoving to get it open this time. For a moment, Nancy was afraid it had locked behind them accidentally. But then the door gave, and they sneaked out of the chapel.

Walking into the back quad, they tried to look like ordinary students. The few people who passed didn't give them a second look.

Nancy pointed to the pile of rubble in the back quad. "Look, under that canvas sheet," she said. "There's all the workers' equipment."

"I'm sure they won't mind if we borrow a tool or two," George said with a grin.

Bess and George kept lookout while Nancy ducked under the canvas. As she rummaged around in the dark, her hand struck a smooth, long iron shape. A crowbar!

Nancy grabbed the crowbar and slipped it under her cotton sweater. Part of it stuck out at the bottom, but she held her purse over it. Walking nonchalantly, the girls returned to the chapel. They slipped through the door, leaving it ajar.

Nancy slipped the fork of the crowbar into the broken mortar. Wedging the corner of the stone, she pried it up a couple of inches. Bess and George, kneeling, grabbed the lifted stone. Nancy put aside the crowbar and helped them. They slowly raised the flat block of stone.

Underneath lay a base of mossy bricks. And on top of them lay a long white envelope.

"Nancy, that must be it!" George said.

Nancy picked up the envelope. She turned it over. A blob of black wax held down the flap. Pressed into the flap was the shape of a rose.

Nancy slid her finger under the flap and broke the seal. She opened the envelope.

Inside was a folded sheet of stiff paper. Nancy unfolded it. After slipping her penlight from her purse, she pored over the loopy black script.

"Is that Miss Innes's handwriting?" Bess asked. "It doesn't look like the writing on the riddle."

Nancy shook her head. Her hands trembled slightly with excitement. "This wasn't written by Dorothy Innes," she said. "It was written by Dame Gwyneth Davies. And it looks like a will!"

George seized Bess's arm. "A will!" she exclaimed. "Read it, Nan!"

"Well, not a will, precisely," Nancy said. "It's a codicil—a paper that amends certain parts of her original will. The date is only three months ago. She probably wrote this a few weeks before she died." Nancy looked up solemnly. "This may well reflect Dame Gwyneth's last wishes."

"But what does it say?" Bess asked.

Nancy trained her penlight on the codicil. " 'I,

Gwyneth Davies, being of sound mind and body, do hereby amend my last will and testament,' " she read. " 'I bequeath the entire proceeds from my play *The Monkey Puzzle* to my godson, Anthony D'Souza.' "

"Tony D'Souza!" George exclaimed. "He's Gwyneth Davies's godson?"

"That explains the black rose signets!" Nancy said, snapping her fingers. "Dame Gwyneth must have given matching rings to her grandson, Simon, and her godson, Tony."

"But Tony told you it came from his dead mother," George pointed out.

"That's what he said," Nancy said. "Either he's lying, or he didn't know the truth. After his mother died, maybe his father didn't even tell him he had a godmother."

"The entire proceeds of *The Monkey Puzzle*," Bess said, still looking amazed. "Wow. Didn't Pippa say that the play is a monster hit?"

"You bet," Nancy said. "It could make Tony very rich indeed."

"Oh, I hope it's true," George said. "Do you think this codicil is legitimate, Nancy?"

"I'm no expert," Nancy said. "But remember what Dad said in his lecture tonight? In America and in Great Britain, a duly attested will or codicil overrules any earlier wills. And this has been signed by a witness—it's the St. Cyril's porter, Albert Godwin," she read, peering at the signature. "If Mr. Godwin can testify that Dame Gwyneth was sane when she wrote this, I think the courts would accept it."

"It may also help that it's handwritten," Bess added. "I remember that from your dad's lecture. If the handwriting is shown to be hers, that would prove that this reflects her wishes—that somebody else didn't write it and force her to sign it."

"We need to turn this over to Dame Gwyneth's lawyers," Nancy said. "We'll have to ask Mr. Godwin about it, too. If all goes well, in a few months Tony D'Souza could be rich!"

"Not if I can help it." A voice spoke from the shadows near the chapel door.

Simon Coningsby stepped into the moonlight, still dressed in his black doublet and tights from the play.

He was carrying a dagger.

"Hand over that paper," he told Nancy curtly.

Nancy tried to stall. "This?" she asked, waving the codicil. "Oh, it's nothing important."

"Don't pull that on me," Simon said with a sneer. "I was listening at the door long enough to know better. I've been looking for that paper. Surely you don't think I'd let Tony D'Souza rob me of my rightful fortune, do you?"

"I'd forgotten that *you* were Dame Gwyneth's heir," Bess said.

"Indeed I am—and I mean to keep it that way," Simon said. "Your friend Tony will never know the difference. He doesn't even know that my grandmother was his godmother."

"So she really was?" Nancy asked.

Simon gave a scoffing laugh. "My grandmother was so softhearted. Twenty years ago she had pneumonia and hired a home nurse named Shanta D'Souza. Somehow they became fond of each other. When Mrs. D'Souza had a baby a year later, Grandmum agreed to be its godmother. I got the whole story a few years ago from Mrs. Kelly, Grandmum's housekeeper. She's the one who raised me after my parents died."

"But then your grandmother lost touch with Tony?" Nancy asked.

"Either that, or she lost interest," Simon said, waving the dagger casually. "After all, I was born a few months later—the only son of her only daughter. Who needed a godson when she had such a brilliant grandson?"

"But she didn't totally lose interest in Tony," Nancy said. "She gave him a black rose signet ring, just like yours."

Simon looked startled for a second. "She did?"

"He's wearing it now," Nancy said.

"So that's why you asked about my ring the other night at the play," Simon said, pointing the tip of the dagger toward Nancy.

"I think it's nice she left Tony something," Bess said meekly.

"Nice!" Simon said, swinging toward Bess. "Grandmum didn't do it to be nice to Tony—she did it to punish *me*. When I was growing up, she was always on at me. 'Why are your marks so bad in school? Why are your manners so rude? I've spoilt you too badly.'"

Good for Dame Gwyneth, Nancy thought grimly to herself. Now that she saw Simon's true colors, she disliked him intensely.

"We had our last fight—a real blowup—just before she died," Simon said. "She threatened to cut me off without a penny. 'That will build your character if nothing else will!' she said. I stormed back to Oxford in a rage. She fell ill that night. But it wasn't until a week later that I learned she was dying. I rushed back, hoping to reconcile with her, but she was unconscious by the time I arrived. She died two hours later."

"You already knew she was leaving everything to you, of course," Nancy said.

"Of course," he said. "But after she died, Mrs. Kelly told me Grandmum had asked Dorothy Innes to come over the day after our fight. They spent some time chattering together, and Mrs. Kelly overheard Grandmum say something about an important paper. That worried me—Miss Innes has never liked me. I felt sure Grandmum had written a new will disinheriting me."

"And you suspected that Miss Innes knew where it was," George said.

Simon swiveled toward George. "I knew she did!" he said with a snarl. "At first I thought I was safe. The lawyers only had the old will, and everything went as expected. But I was afraid Dorothy Innes would ruin it all. I had to keep her quiet. Of course, it was easy intimidating an old woman in a wheelchair. Anonymous phone calls, threatening notes, ugly presents on her doorstep—I had her sewn up. Until you snoops arrived."

He took a threatening step toward Nancy.

"You may have terrorized her, but Miss Innes is too tough to give in," Nancy said. "She found a way to get us interested in the case, without letting you see her talking to us."

"Did she really think I'd be fooled by that arrow?" Simon scoffed. "I knew she was an expert archer, and it didn't take me long to figure out that she'd set you on the trail. At first I tried to stop you. I didn't want anyone finding that will! But you kept on looking." He laughed grimly. "So I simply followed you until you led me here."

He gestured with the dagger. "And now that you have the will, you'd better hand it over—or else."

16

A Puzzle Solved

The dagger glinted in Simon's hand.

Nancy's jaw set stubbornly. Her steady blue eyes met his desperate gray eyes. "Maybe you can intimidate an elderly woman in a wheelchair," she said, "but you can't scare me. You haven't got the nerve to stick that knife in me."

"Just try me," Simon replied in a deadly snarl. He took another step closer to Nancy, jabbing the dagger toward her throat.

Suddenly, the door swung open with a loud creak. Pippa and Tony burst into the chapel.

Thrown off guard, Simon pivoted, waving the knife wildly. Nancy leaped toward him, grabbing his wrist. She wrested the dagger from him, and it fell with a clatter on the stone floor. Bess scrambled to pick it up.

Tony and George tackled Simon from behind,

pinning him to the floor. "I'll go call Inspector Morris," Pippa said. She turned and ran out.

"How did you know we were here?" Nancy asked Tony.

"Your father went home with Mr. Shaw for a cup of coffee after his lecture," Tony said. "When he saw Pippa, he told her your latest hunch about the rose. She phoned me and suggested we join you here. We knew something was up when we saw the cloak from Simon's costume on the chapel steps. He must have come here straight from the play."

"He brought something else from the play, too," Bess said. "This dagger—it's just a stage prop." She demonstrated how the blade retracted harmlessly into the handle.

"An empty threat—thank goodness," Nancy said.

Simon closed his eyes and turned his head. "I had to try something," he said in a voice choked with emotion. "This new will—it disinherits me. I couldn't bear being a penniless orphan, not after being rich all my life. And to see that upstart lording it over me—" He opened his eyes and shot a look of hatred at Tony.

"But most of Dame Gwyneth's fortune is still yours," Nancy said. "This is only a codicil. Tony inherits only the profits from *The Monkey Puzzle*."

Simon wrenched his head around to stare at Nancy, horrified. "Only *The Monkey Puzzle*? You mean I risked all this . . ." He buried his face and groaned.

"Who inherits the profits from *The Monkey Puzzle?*" Tony asked slowly, stunned.

George dropped a friendly hand on Tony's shoulder. "Tony," she said with a smile, "have we got a story to tell you."

"I can't believe you managed to get us box seats, Tony!" Bess exclaimed.

Tony smiled bashfully. "The lawyers will need time to decide whether I am Gwyneth Davies's heir," he said, "but the theater manager has no doubts. And when I told him my friends wanted to see *The Monkey Puzzle,* right away he offered me the royal box."

Settling down on a red velvet seat, Nancy gazed around the ornate private balcony. "We couldn't ask for better seats," she said.

Tony had invited Nancy, Bess, George, Pippa, Mr. Drew, and Miss Innes to the theater, as a way of celebrating his sudden good fortune. They had all taken the train together from Oxford down to London. The four Americans would be flying home from the London airport the next day.

"Well, you girls deserve a treat, after the splendid sleuthing you did," Miss Innes said, deftly positioning her wheelchair in the box. "I certainly picked the right detectives to do my legwork."

"We know why you didn't approach us

directly—you were being threatened by Simon," George said. "But why couldn't you have given us more clues?"

"I didn't have any more clues myself," Miss Innes said. "When I last saw Gwyneth Davies, her mind was wandering. I gathered that she was furious with Simon—and rightly so, I might add. A bad piece of work, that young fellow."

"His actions over the past week have proved that," Mr. Drew said.

"Gwyneth told me only that an important paper was hidden 'behind a black rose' in Oxford," Miss Innes said. "She said she'd hidden it there a week earlier, even before her fight with Simon. I think she was tormented about cutting Simon out of even part of his inheritance. Until they fought, she wasn't certain that she wanted the codicil found. But then she did."

"But why entrust it to you?" Bess asked.

"Once a Puzzler, always a Puzzler," Miss Innes said, tapping Bess's arm with her theater program. "Even on that slim clue, she knew I'd try to find the document and bring it to light. The trouble was, I didn't try right away."

"I don't blame you," Pippa said. "You were grieving for your friend."

Miss Innes shrugged. "Maybe at first," she said. "But truth to tell, I wasn't certain there really was such a paper—not until I started receiving the threatening calls and notes."

"Did you guess that it was Simon threatening you?" Mr. Drew asked her.

"Not at first," she admitted. "None of the threats mentioned Gwyneth or the black rose, so I was mystified. Once I realized what he was after, I guessed his identity. But I couldn't turn him in to the police. I had no definite proof it was he."

"So your only course was to find the black rose," Nancy said.

"Yes," Miss Innes said. "But I felt rather helpless. How could I search properly, stuck in this thing?" She slapped the wheel of her wheelchair.

"That's where Nancy came in," Pippa said.

"Right," Miss Innes said. "When I learned you were a detective, Miss Drew, I set to work. I went back to my rooms and fetched my bow and arrow. I tore that drama poster from a bulletin board in the passage. The fact that it was advertising Simon's play seemed a stroke of good luck to me. I thought perhaps it might steer you onto his trail."

"It did, somewhat," Nancy said.

"I composed my riddle, then I took the elevator up to the minstrel's gallery and shot the arrow," Miss Innes went on. "I thought such a ploy would grab your attention—as well as protect both of us."

"That way, the person threatening you wouldn't link Nancy with the case," Mr. Drew said, "and he wouldn't punish you for passing on the information."

"But it didn't work," George said, leaning back

in her seat. "The arrow must have alerted Simon to Nancy's involvement. That's why he stopped to talk to us Wednesday morning in the Junior Common Room."

"And I thought he was flirting with me," Bess said. She sounded slightly let down. "But he must have seen us scheming with Tony over the Wycherly manuscript. That's why Simon tried to steal it from Miss Innes's rooms—and why he made the threatening phone call to Pippa."

"It didn't sound like him on the phone," Pippa said, "but as an actor, Simon probably had no trouble disguising his voice."

"Remember that we saw him at the restaurant Wednesday night?" George said. "He probably eavesdropped on us and learned about the rose in the Fellows' Garden. So he came along and knocked Bess out with the chloroform. Borrowed from a friend who's studying biology, I'll bet."

"And Thursday, when we went punting, he followed us on a bike so he could tamper with our punt pole," Pippa said.

"He was extra busy on Friday," Nancy said. "He must have hidden outside our hotel and saw George and Bess go off with Mrs. Cole. He followed me to the library, then to my meeting with Tony."

"I guess he couldn't resist shoving me out of the tower," Tony said with a nervous grin.

"He drove straight out to the Cotswolds after that," Nancy said. "He probably knew which stables Mrs. Cole uses. I checked—Simon does drive a black sports car, just like the one that spooked your horse, George."

"I spoke to Mr. Cole before we left, by the way," Mr. Drew said. "He said to tell you he was sorry he didn't take your case seriously."

"In the end, it didn't matter," Nancy said. "The rose wasn't hidden in Boniface anyway."

"No, it was in St. Cyril's all the time," Bess said. "The funny thing is, it was Simon who led us to it, in a way. If he hadn't pushed the block of stone over the wall at us, we'd never have gone inside St. Cyril's in the first place."

"That's true, Bess," Nancy said. "I should have realized it wasn't a coincidence that Simon showed up a few minutes later, eager to help us investigate that falling stone."

"And then he was the one who actually turned us on to the rose window," Bess said. "How ironic. Of course, he didn't know any more than we did that it was the rose we wanted."

"That was the day we met Mr. Godwin, the porter," Nancy added. "Who, by the way, was Dame Gwyneth's old pal. He's the one who witnessed the codicil."

"Mr. Godwin has verified that Dame Gwyneth wrote the codicil," Mr. Drew said. "She told him not to say a word about it to anyone, and she never told him where she had hidden it. His testimony will help settle the case more quickly. In Tony's favor, of course."

"Dame Gwyneth must have slipped the envelope

under the stone when the workers were repairing the chapel floor," Nancy murmured. "I bet she was thrilled to find such a clever hiding place."

"Tony, did you really have no idea you were Gwyneth's godson?" Miss Innes asked, laying a hand on his arm.

"Not a clue," Tony admitted. "My father never mentioned it. When I first came to Boniface, Simon must have latched on to me so he could work out how much I knew. Once he realized I had no idea she was my godmother, he dropped me."

"Simon must have gone bonkers when he saw us chatting with Tony in the Junior Common Room," Pippa said with a giggle. "I imagine he thought Miss Innes had told Tony who his godmother was."

"I didn't dare do that, of course," Miss Innes said. "Not with all those threats aimed at me. I didn't want to put Tony in danger, too."

"I hope Simon won't go to prison," Tony said.

"He'll be charged with several crimes," Mr. Drew said. He ticked them off on his fingers. "Harassment, breaking and entering, and reckless endangerment. Depending on the jury, he may well spend a few years in prison."

"The end of a brilliant acting career," Bess said with a sigh. "What a pity. Simon is so talented— and so handsome."

"It *is* ironic," Miss Innes said as the theater lights began to go down. "Simon will still be wealthy from his grandmother's other royalties. He had no need to worry about the small portion that will be going to Tony."

"It might be small to him," Tony said, lowering his voice as the audience hushed. "But it will change my life completely."

"Nancy, look," Pippa whispered as the curtain rose. "In that vase on the stage—a black rose!"

"Trust Gwyneth Davies to stick a black rose in her play," Nancy whispered to Miss Innes. "You were right—once a Puzzler, always a Puzzler."

Miss Innes patted Nancy's hand. "Welcome to the Puzzlers, my dear," she whispered. "I can't think of anyone who deserves to be a member more than Nancy Drew."

Meet up with suspense and mystery in

FRANK AND JOE HARDY:

#1 The Gross Ghost Mystery
Frank and Joe are making friends and meeting monsters!

#2 The Karate Clue
Somebody's kicking up a major mess!

#3 First Day, Worst Day
Everybody's mad at Joe! Is he a tattletale?

#4 Jump Shot Detectives
He shoots! He scores! He steals?

#5 Dinosaur Disaster
It's big, it's bad, it's a Bayport-asaurus! Sort-of.

By Franklin W. Dixon

1398-04